ATHLETE VS. MATHLETE

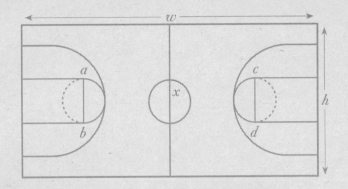

ATHLETE vs.
MATHLETE

W. C. Mack

SCHOLASTIC INC.

ISBN 978-0-545-60416-1

12 11 10 9 8 7 6 5 4 3 2   14 15 16 17 18/0

Printed in the U.S.A.   40

First Scholastic printing, May 2013

Book design by Nicole Gastonguay

For the boys: Tyler, Colten, Joey, and Christian
And for Mike, superfan of the 1976–77 World Champion
Portland Trail Blazers

ATHLETE vs. MATHLETE

OWEN

Tip-off

Seventh-grade basketball started out all wrong, and it only got worse.

"He wants us to *try out*?" Chris asked.

"Unbelievable," I muttered, staring at the sign-up sheet on our new coach's office door.

Try out for our own team?

Chris, the rest of the guys, and I had been playing together since Cotter Elementary. We were undefeated in sixth grade (if you didn't count our five losses, which I didn't because the refs had been out to get us), and we'd been shooting hoops at Sunset Park all summer to stay on top of our game.

"Next Wednesday afternoon," Chris said, then pointed at the word as he read it. *"Tryouts."*

I shook my head. "This is nuts."

"Yeah, but what can we do about it?"

"Talk to the coach," I said, knocking on his door.

"Come in," a deep voice boomed from inside the office.

"You coming?" I asked Chris, hoping I had backup.

"Uh . . ." He took a couple of steps away from me.

"I guess that's a no." I rolled my eyes, turned the knob, and swung the door open.

I only knew three facts about our new coach:

1. He was from North Carolina.
2. He loved to win.
3. He wanted us to try out for our own team.

And when I walked into his office . . .

4. He was a freakin' giant.

Seriously, like thirteen feet tall. And it was all muscle.

Before I could say anything, I heard Chris breathing next to me. *Whew*. I wasn't facing the beast alone.

"Hi," I said to Coach Baxter. It sounded like a squeak, so I cleared my throat and tried again. "Hi, Coach."

"What can I do for you?" he asked, without looking up from the box of books he was unpacking.

I checked out the team photos on the wall behind his

desk, the framed newspaper pages with "champ" headlines, and the shiny trophies on top of his bookcase.

The guy obviously knew what he was doing. But so did we, the Lewis and Clark Middle School Pioneers.

"The clock is ticking," Coach Baxter growled.

I cleared my throat again. "Uh . . . it's about the tryouts."

Coach lined up the books on the middle shelf, from tallest to shortest. "Next Wednesday at three."

"Yeah. I saw the sign, but I wanted to talk to you about it because—"

"You can't make it? Tough break." He reached into the box for more books. "It's Wednesday at three. No exceptions."

Chris elbowed me and whispered, "Let's go."

But I wasn't finished. "I can make it. I just don't think I *need* to."

Coach Baxter finally looked at me, and I wished he hadn't. His eyes were like death rays. "And why is that?" he asked, standing up straight and crossing his arms over his chest.

I was way off. He was probably closer to fourteen feet tall.

"Because I was on the team last year, and—"

"It's a new year," he interrupted.

"I know, but Coach Miller—"

"I'm the new coach."

"Yeah, but the Pioneers—"

"It's a new team."

Getting a whole sentence out of my mouth would have been awesome. "I get that, but—"

"I don't think you do," he said, dropping into his chair. "What's your name?"

"Uh-oh," Chris whispered.

"Owen Evans."

"Listen, Owen. I'm in charge, and I'll pick my team the way I want to. Nobody gets a jersey just because they played last year. I'm sorry if you don't like it, but that's the way it is." He looked us over. "Any questions?"

Chris and I both gulped.

"Okay, then I'll see you next Wednesday, ready to work."

"Sure." I nodded, and Chris pushed me out the door.

Once we were back in the hallway, I groaned, "This totally stinks."

We grabbed our stuff from our lockers, and I saw my brother, Russell, coming our way. He was carrying more books than any other kid in the hallway and his glasses were sliding down his nose, like they always did. He stopped to fix the top book on his stack and ended up dropping the whole pile on the floor.

"I can't believe you guys are related," Chris said, shaking his head.

No one could. We were twins, but *nobody* ever believed

it, even when we said we were fraternal, not identical. Russell and I are totally different. He's almost five inches taller than I am and has arms like wet spaghetti. Even in his brown cords, his legs look like toothpicks and his crazy curly hair is nothing like mine.

"Hey, Russ," I said, picking up a couple of books and handing them to him.

"Thanks," Russ said, smiling.

That was another difference between us. Russ never let stuff bug him, and I got mad a couple of times a day, minimum. Mom said I was a short fuse and he was a slow boil. The thing is, my brother never actually boiled over. Like, ever.

He checked his digital watch. "I'm late for class. I'll see you at home," he said, heading for the stairs.

"Hey, you!" a voice boomed from behind us.

It sounded like a jet flying too low, but instead of ducking, I turned around and saw Coach Baxter waving one arm in the air. It was like watching King Kong take over the hallway, and I was surprised he didn't have a school bus full of screaming kids in one hand and a freaked-out librarian in the other.

Everyone was looking around, trying to see who he was yelling at.

"Tall kid!" Coach shouted.

The only one who hadn't bothered to look was my brother.

"Do you mean Russell?" I asked, totally confused.

"Who's Russell?" he barked at me.

"That skinny kid over there," I said, pointing. "He's my twin."

Coach turned to stare at me.

"Fraternal," I explained, then shouted, "Hey, Russ!"

That stopped him. My brother turned around, and I waved him over.

He had to fight the crowd, and when he finally got to us, his face was red and he was out of breath, like the spawning salmon we learned about in science class. "Yes?"

"Coach wants to talk to you," I told him.

"He does?" When Russ turned to Coach, his eyes bugged out, like he hadn't noticed there was a giant standing there. Like you couldn't see the guy from outer space.

"You play?" Coach asked.

Russell looked as confused as I was. "Play what?"

"Basketball," Coach said.

Chris and I both cracked up.

"What's so funny?" Coach snapped.

That shut us up, and he looked at my brother again. "I want you to come to tryouts next week."

Russ just stared at him. "Are you talking about *basketball* tryouts?"

"No, ballet," Coach growled.

Russ blinked hard. "I'm sorry. I don't—"

"*Of course* I mean basketball."

"Uh . . ." Russell looked at me as if I knew what was happening, but I had no idea.

Russell? Basketball? It had to be a joke.

"I think I'm going to need someone your height," Coach said.

"My height?" Russ asked.

Coach stared into his eyes, like he was trying to figure out if there was something wrong with him. "Yes. You're the tallest kid at this school, and you'd be perfect at center."

Center? *Paul* played center!

"But I'm on the honor roll," Russell said.

"And athletes can't be good students?" Coach asked.

"No."

"Thanks a lot," I muttered.

"I disagree," Coach said. "And I want to see you there next Wednesday."

"But I—" Russell started.

Coach lifted a hand in the air to stop him. "This isn't a request, uh . . . what's your name again?"

"Russell Evans." My brother sighed just like he did when Mom got him the wrong periodic-table T-shirt.

Like there was a *right* one.

"Mr. Evans," Coach said, "I'll see you at tryouts next Wednesday."

I watched Coach disappear into his office and wondered

if he was totally nuts. My brother was seriously the worst athlete on the planet. He couldn't even dribble! He tripped over a soccer ball in second grade and broke his arm. He hit himself in the face with his own badminton racket. He was a perfect fit for the library, not the locker room.

Russ frowned. "So, I guess I'll be making a complete fool of myself next Wednesday. Everyone knows I'm smart, not sporty."

"*Athletic,*" I groaned. "No one says 'sporty.'"

Russell nodded. "But you understand what I'm saying, don't you? Everyone knows you're the jock and I'm the brains. I'll feel like a joke if I go."

The fact was, he *would* be a joke. And the bigger mess he made of tryouts, the more I'd hear about it. Would the guys make fun of me, too, knowing Russ and I shared DNA? Probably. And that was the last thing I wanted to deal with.

I shook my head and an idea popped into it. An awesome idea. "Don't worry about it, Russ. We'll practice this weekend so you'll be ready."

Chris was looking at me like I was crazy. "That's a long shot," he whispered.

"Cool beans," my brother said, nodding.

"No, it's just cool, Russ."

"Okay, *cool.*" He smiled.

As usual, there was something brown and gooey stuck in his braces.

"Look," I said. "There's no way you'll make the team."

"No way," Chris echoed.

"Not a chance." Russell laughed.

"But I promise to make tryouts as painless as possible." For him *and* for me.

"Thanks, Owen," he said, lifting his hand to give me a high five.

He missed.

"Did you get your practice schedule yet?" Dad asked me at the dinner table that night.

"Nope," I said, shaking my head. "We have to make the team before we can practice."

"Make the team?" Mom asked. "You're already—"

"The new coach is making us try out."

"Wow," Dad said, passing me the chicken. "That's different."

"Yeah, different and stupid."

"*Hmm.*" Dad raised his eyebrows. "That might be the only time I've ever heard you use the word 'stupid' to describe basketball."

"Because it's totally stupid. I was already on the team!"

"Maybe your new coach wants to shake things up a little," Dad said.

Coach Baxter wasn't just "shaking things up a little." He

was causing a freakin' earthquake. "Yeah, right. He wants *Russell* to try out."

Dad was reaching for the rice but he froze. He looked at my twin. "Is that true?"

"I guess," Russ said, through a mouthful of green beans that would probably be stuck in his braces for the next four days.

"Well, that's great news," Dad said, slapping him on the back.

Russ almost choked. "I won't make it," he said.

"Who told you that?" Dad asked.

Russell looked at me and I shrugged.

"Owen?" Mom said, all disappointed. "That's not very nice."

"I wasn't trying to be mean," I told her. "He won't, and he's cool with that. Right, Russ?"

Both of my parents looked at my brother, waiting for an answer.

"I don't care," he told them. "Making the basketball team isn't exactly a goal of mine."

"I'm lost," Mom said.

"Coach Baxter is forcing him to try out," I explained. "He says he needs Russ's height at center."

"I can see that," Dad said, nodding slowly.

"Wait a second," Mom said. "The coach is *forcing* him to try out?"

"I think it's a great idea," Dad said, taking a bite of his chicken. "Are you ready for it, Russ?"

"Owen's going to practice with me."

Dad smiled at me. "I can help you guys out. We can run some drills on Saturday, then get a pickup game going in the park on Sunday."

"What?" I gulped.

"Uh, I have a Masters of the Mind meeting on Saturday," Russ said.

"Masters of the Mind," Dad mumbled, probably trying to remember what that was. "Can't you cancel?"

Russ's eyes bulged open, like he had a chicken bone jammed in his throat.

"What?" Dad asked, shrugging. "Basketball tryouts are once a year."

"So is the Masters of the Mind district competition," Russ told him. "It's only three weeks away."

"And his team is depending on him," Mom said, shooting Dad the kind of look none of us wanted to get.

"Exactly," Russ said. "This could be our year, if we find the right replacement for Chao. Of course, we've got an excellent team already. Nitu is a math wizard and—"

"More wizards?" I laughed. "What was that wizard book you wouldn't put down a couple of weeks ago?"

"*Gruden's Path*." Russ grinned. "It's about a third-circle wizard who wants to become a Golden—"

"Okay, okay," Dad said, holding up a hand to stop him before all our heads exploded. "Go to your meeting on Saturday, and we'll practice on Sunday." He nodded, like it was settled, then winked at Russ. "This is going to be a lot of fun."

I wasn't so sure.

The Undiscovered Element

I didn't even mention basketball tryouts to my Masters of the Mind team because we had bigger issues to deal with. Our most artistic member, Chao Liu, had recently moved to Cincinnati, and I could practically smell the panic at our afternoon meeting.

"We're doomed," Jason Schmidt said, chewing on his thumbnail.

Of course, Jason thought he was doomed when the lunch ladies sprinkled cheese on his chili.

"At least we're still close to him alphabetically," Sara said hopefully. "You know, Ohio and Oregon."

I wasn't sure how that would help, but I appreciated her effort.

Jason groaned. "We're *doomed*."

"We're not doomed," I told him. "We'll figure this out. After all, we're brainstorming experts."

"Please don't tell me to put my thinking cap on, Russell," Jason said, and sighed. "I can't take it. I mean, this is serious."

"I know it's serious." I looked each of my three teammates in the eye. "But all we really need to do is find someone else."

"Yeah, and convince 'someone else' that Masters of the Mind is cool," Nitu said.

"It *is* cool," I reminded her.

"*We* know that," Sara said, "but everybody else thinks it's a geek convention."

"No, they don't," I told her.

"Actually, they do, Russell," Nitu said, shrugging as she played with the tip of her long black braid. "But I don't care. I love this team."

"So do I." I nodded. "And so will our new member."

"I feel weird about this," Sara said, quietly. "Chao was our friend."

"And we'll make another friend," I promised. "You have to trust me." And they did, too. I was team leader. "I'm sure there are tons of Lewis and Clark students who'll jump at the chance to compete."

"You really think so?" Jason asked doubtfully.

"We did," I reminded him.

"That's true." Nitu nodded. "I was dying to join Masters of the Mind as soon as I saw the booth on Club Day."

"My brother was on the team for three years," Sara said. "I used to watch his competitions and daydream about my turn."

I thought of the basketball team, whose members only cared about throwing a ball through a hoop, and shook my head. "So, should we get started with a warm-up?"

We agreed on a rhyming animal drill and Nitu began with, "Would a gray dog disappear in the fog?"

"Not bad," Sara said, smiling. "Does an arctic fox need winter socks?"

"Do healthy parrots eat peas and carrots?" I asked.

We waited for Jason, but he was silent.

"Your turn," Nitu said.

He frowned. "I'm trying to think of something that rhymes with squirrel."

"Seriously?" Nitu groaned. "There's a whole animal kingdom out there, Jason."

"Fine." He closed his eyes for a second, then asked, "Would a bath stop a monkey from smelling funky?"

We got on a roll from there.

"Do teenage rabbits have nasty habits?"

"Is a funny giraffe good for a laugh?"

"Do tired sheep have to stand while they sleep?"

"Would a hungry ape peel a grape?"

"Can a lonely dove fall in love?"

We kept our rhythm for several minutes until I asked, "Would a bear care to share his lair?"

Nitu gave me a sly smile. "Four at once, huh?"

"I can top that," Jason said. "Would a big pig in a wig eat a fig?"

"Okay, that's still four." Sara laughed. "Would mice find two lice twice as nice?"

"Four again." Nitu thought for a second or two. "If a rat sat on a fat cat's mat, would the cat be okay with that, or find a bat to go after the brat?"

"Show off." I groaned.

"She said 'cat' twice," Jason quickly pointed out.

"Remember the time Chao rhymed eleven words?" Sara asked, smiling.

Everyone was quiet, and I knew we were all missing him.

"He's not going to be easy to replace," Nitu said.

"I asked Adam Johnson to join the team and he laughed in my face," Jason said.

"Same with Becky Harper." Sara sighed. "And I really thought she'd be into it."

Jason moaned. "We're doomed."

"Look," I said, ready to move on. "I don't think we're going to find someone in Sara's living room in the next forty-five minutes, so maybe we should work on something else. Like one of the older questions?"

When Sara found the right page in her binder, we listened as she read a question out loud.

"*Hmm,*" Nitu said when she finished. "*When does one equal two?*"

We were quiet for a few seconds. I could hear Sara's mom in the kitchen, which made me think of my own mom, and I came up with the first answer.

"Twins. One pregnancy equals two babies."

"Nice one," Sara said, grinning.

"How about yams and sweet potatoes?" Jason asked. "One vegetable, two names."

"They aren't the same thing," Sara told him, shaking her head. "Yams have more natural sugar in them, and more moisture."

"Why do you know that?" Nitu asked, laughing.

Sara smiled and raised an eyebrow. "Why do you know the first twenty decimal places of pi?"

"Twenty-five," our math whiz said, grinning. "And good point."

"Okay." Sara stared at the ceiling. "When does one equal two?"

"I know," Jason said, snapping his fingers. "Basketball. One basket equals two points."

"Hey," I said, thinking of my strange experience at

school. "You won't believe this, but Coach Baxter is making *me* try out for the basketball team."

Everyone froze.

"Why?" Jason finally asked.

"I'm tall." I shrugged.

"Sure, but . . . ," Nitu said, then cringed.

"Tall is one thing," Jason said, shaking his head, "but you don't *play*."

"I'm aware of that."

"What will you have to do?" he asked, looking worried. "Run?"

I shrugged. "Run, jump, and shoot, I guess."

"Russ, can you do *any* of those things?" he asked, looking doubtful.

"Not very well," I admitted.

"Me neither," Nitu said. "And all three at once? Yeah, right."

"So, tryouts will be over quickly. I'll try, fail, and be done with it."

I didn't feel the slightest bit offended when everyone nodded.

"Okay, so Russell has shared *his* news," Nitu said, with a smile. "Isn't anyone going to ask me about *mine*?"

"Okay," Jason said, "what's your . . . oh, the district competition!"

"Yes." Nitu pulled out a blue piece of paper and cleared

her throat. "This year's challenge is to drop an egg from a two-story window onto the pavement below, without a break or a crack."

I could practically hear the pistol go off so our minds could start racing.

Nitu continued, "We get six rubber bands; a piece of Styrofoam; one roll each of aluminum foil, duct tape, and plastic wrap; ten feet of string; ten newspaper pages; four chopsticks—"

"What are we supposed to do with chopsticks?" Jason asked.

"Let her finish," I whispered.

"Three cups of water," Nitu continued, "a plastic margarine container, a pair of scissors, and two toilet-paper tubes."

When she was done, we all sat back to think.

"What about wrapping the egg in the foil?" Jason suggested.

"And?" Nitu prompted.

"That's it. If it's wrapped thick enough."

"This is Masters of the Mind," Nitu reminded him. "The best and brightest."

"And?" Jason asked.

"And you're seriously suggesting a ball of foil?"

"Remember, we have to use more than *five* of the items," Sara added.

At that moment, Mrs. Phillips walked into the living

room with our snack. As the Masters of the Mind team worked our way through a dozen sugar cookies and two dozen ideas in the next forty-five minutes, I couldn't help wondering who was going to fill our fifth spot. The district competition was only three weeks away.

And that wasn't the only thing I was worried about.

Basketball tryouts were guaranteed to be a waste of time, and time wasn't something I had a lot of. I had a paper due for English class, a math quiz that week, and the school librarian told me I was next on the list to borrow Franz Helsen's new book. I'd have it on Friday, and I wanted to read it straight through the weekend.

Why did Coach have to choose me?

"I'd better head for home," Nitu said, interrupting my thoughts.

"I should go, too," Jason said, grabbing his big black case. "Tuba practice."

I slipped the straps of my backpack onto my shoulders. "So, we'll meet on Saturday at your house, right?" I asked Nitu.

"Ten o'clock," she said, nodding.

"And next Wednesday we're at your place, Russell?" Sara asked.

"No. I've got those basketball tryouts."

"Wait, they're on *Wednesday*?" Jason gasped.

"Yes."

"But we're meeting next Wednesday instead of our usual Thursday," Nitu said. "Thursday's my dad's birthday. Remember?"

Actually, I'd forgotten. "Yes, but—"

"Hold on," Jason interrupted. "We're down to *four* team members, and now we're losing Russell? We're doomed."

"I'm not leaving the team," I told him. "I'm just missing one practice."

No one spoke right away.

"Obviously we need you at the meetings," Nitu finally said, "but one without you won't kill us."

I felt my shoulders relax.

"You're *sure* it'll be just one, though?" Jason asked, still sounding worried.

"Definitely," I told him.

Nitu laughed. "He's trying out for basketball, not *Jeopardy!*, Jason. There's only one way this could turn out."

"That's right," I said, laughing. "After Wednesday, my schedule will be back to normal."

"Russell?" Sara asked, glancing up from the Masters of the Mind binder. "What if you make it?"

"Make what?" I asked, confused.

"The team," she said, softly.

We all started laughing at once.

"Sara," I said when I caught my breath. "There's no way I'll make the team."

OWEN

Personal Foul

I got my second taste of the giant in PE on Friday.

"I'm Coach Baxter," he said in that booming voice. "Welcome to my class."

When I looked at the guys' faces, I could tell which ones hadn't seen him before. Their mouths were hanging open in total shock.

But I was a step ahead of them. I'd already decided that gym-class basketball was an awesome chance to show Coach my moves before tryouts.

We split up into teams, and I moved to center court for the tip-off. It wasn't my usual position, so I'd be showing Coach how flexible I was.

He stood next to me and Paul, who was playing center for the other team. When the ball was tossed, I went for it.

My fingers hit it first, and I pushed the ball toward Nicky Chu. He caught it and pivoted fast before passing it to Nate James. Nate was the fastest guy on the Pioneers, and he made a breakaway, dribbling toward the basket.

The rest of us ran hard to keep up, and I was glad I'd done so much jogging in the summer. Right when he got to the hoop, Nate looked left, then passed to me.

As soon as I had the ball, I lined up the shot and took it. *Swish.*

Nothing but net!

The guys and I shouted and high-fived. We were on fire already!

Coach blew his whistle. "Good work, but you can't stand around congratulating yourselves every time you score. Get that ball back in play."

He was just as tough for the rest of the scrimmage, even though it was only a gym class. It turned out that Coach wanted to see us sweat buckets. I couldn't remember a time when I'd played harder, even during the semifinals last year.

"Are we being graded on this?" Chris asked, in between breaths.

"Only if we survive," Nate answered.

And I wasn't sure all of us would.

Nicky Chu looked like he needed an oxygen tank . . . or a stretcher.

Paul groaned. "If Coach is this tough in gym class—"

"Don't even say it," I warned him.

"Tryouts will be brutal, for sure," Chris finished, wiping the sweat off his forehead with the back of his hand.

Before we could say anything else, Coach shouted, "If you have enough breath for chitchat, maybe we should crank things up a bit!"

That was enough to shut us up.

When class was over, we shuffled into the locker room, totally wiped out.

"Man, I was going to try out, but forget it," Paul said.

"Me, too," Nicky said, groaning.

"Are you kidding?" I choked.

The team I'd been playing with forever might actually split up?

"Kidding?" Paul snorted. "Dude, that guy is a maniac."

But the Pioneers *needed* Nicky and Paul!

"He's just serious about the game," I told them. I thought about the pictures I'd seen on his desk. "He used to coach high school."

"Yeah, well, this is only middle school," Paul said.

"He's won a bunch of state championships," I told him, remembering the headlines on Coach's wall.

"Yeah, in North Carolina. Big deal."

"Hello? *Michael Jordan* is from North Carolina."

Chris suddenly looked all excited. "Baxter coached Jordan?"

I didn't really say that, but if Coach taught there and Jordan went to school there, it was possible.

Wasn't it?

I just smiled.

"No way," Paul whispered. "That's awesome."

"Michael Jordan?" Nicky asked. "*The* Michael Jordan?"

I nodded.

"Maybe tryouts will be worth it," Paul said. "I mean, if he coached Jordan, the guy's gotta know what he's doing."

"Yeah," Nicky said, nodding slowly. "He might be tough, but that's how you make champions, right?"

"That's right," I told the guys. "And we came pretty close to being champions last year. Maybe Coach Baxter will take us over the top."

"Either him or Russell," Chris said, chuckling.

"What?" Paul turned to stare at me. "Russell's trying out?"

Here we go.

"Wait," Nicky said, "you mean your *brother*, Russell?"

I nodded, hoping they'd drop it.

Yeah, right.

"Can he play?" Nate asked.

"No," Chris said, shaking his head. "Not at all."

"Hey," I growled, getting ticked off. "He's only trying out because Coach is making him."

"Because he's *tall*," Chris explained.

"But he has no coordination," Paul said, laughing. "I saw the kid almost kill himself with a yo-yo in fourth grade."

The rest of the guys cracked up, and my hands slowly balled into fists.

There was no way I'd let Russ make a fool of me . . . I mean *himself*, on Wednesday.

No way.

After dinner on Friday night, Dad put on his Bellows jersey, even though the guy retired like a hundred years ago. I grabbed my old Tim Camden T-shirt, from before he got traded, and put it on while I ran downstairs.

With or without my favorite player, it was game night in Portland! I couldn't wait to see the Blazers rock the Rose Garden.

I got the drinks while Dad made a big bowl of popcorn that was so buttery it looked wet.

"This is gonna be our year," he said, handing me a napkin.

"World championship, here we come!" I practically shouted.

If we made it to the playoffs, anyway.

The truth is, I wasn't totally sure about some of the new

players the Blazers had signed. "I just can't believe they traded Camden," I told Dad, for probably the hundredth time since it happened. "Do you think—"

"Russ!" Dad interrupted, when my brother walked by the doorway. "Come and join us."

What?

Russell didn't watch basketball. He studied, read in his room, or watched weird sci-fi movies in the basement.

My brother froze, like he didn't know what to do.

"Uh, I was just going to start my new Franz Helsen book," he said, holding it up so we could see it. The cover had a bunch of wizards and something that looked way too much like a unicorn on it.

"Franz who?" Dad asked.

"Helsen," Russ said, like we should have heard of him. "It's the seventh book in the series." He started talking faster, so I knew he was excited. "I've been waiting for it since school started."

"You can still read it," Dad said, patting the seat next to him. "Just hang out with us and watch the game for a minute or two first."

I looked at my brother and thought about how the guys in the locker room had laughed when they heard he was trying out for the team.

Hmm.

Even though basketball was my thing with Dad, Russell

should probably learn about the game before tryouts. And knowing something about positions and rules would help when we practiced on the weekend, too.

I moved over so he could sit down, even though it would wreck my view of the action.

Russell squeezed in next to me and reached for some popcorn. He scarfed down his handful like an animal (and I don't mean a magical unicorn). Then he leaned back on the couch like my middle cushion had always been his spot.

"Here we go," Dad said, as the Blazers and Suns lined up for the tip-off.

The Blazers got first possession, and I could tell right away that they were in it to win it. Carl Walters made a three-pointer, then snagged a rebound off the Suns like two seconds later. Walters passed to Jenkins, who passed to one of the new guys, DeShawn Williams, who hit a layup for two.

Dad and I high-fived and I turned to give Russell five, too.

He missed, as usual.

About halfway through an awesome first quarter, the Blazers had a fourteen-point lead.

Dad turned to my brother. "What do you think, Russ?"

"Uh . . . it's good," Russell said.

He was holding his book so tightly, his knuckles were whiter than the rest of him. Like it was taking every bit of his strength not to open it.

Poor Russ.

During the second quarter, I tried to make the game more interesting by telling him who some of the players were and giving a bit of background on them.

"Cool," Russell said, when I told him about the Tim Camden trade.

What?

"No," I said, shaking my head. "Not cool at all."

"But they got two players in exchange for one," Russell pointed out.

Geez, it wasn't about *math*.

"Yeah, one awesome guy for two old guys."

Russ pointed at the TV. "One of the 'old guys' just scored."

"That's right," Dad said, pumping a fist in the air.

I sighed. "I know, but—"

"And I'd like to point out that these *old guys* are just a couple of years younger than I am," Dad added.

"*Exactly*," I agreed. "That's the problem."

"Ouch!" Dad groaned.

"You know what I mean," I told him. "Tim Camden's only been in the league for three years. He hasn't even hit his prime yet. They were nuts to trade him."

Russ reached for more popcorn. "I thought he didn't get along with the other players."

How did he know *that*?

"That's true," Dad said. "And no matter how good a player is, he needs to respect the rest of his team."

"Sure," I said. "But last season we would have lost a bunch of games without Camden. Like when we played the Lakers and he made the three-pointer, right at the buzzer."

"I remember." Dad nodded. "But I also remember how much he cost the team in the second quarter. We could have had a nice lead at the end, if he hadn't been fouling like crazy."

He had a point.

"I like that DeShawn Williams," Russ said. "I think the Trail Blazers—"

"Blazers," I corrected. "Fans just say Blazers."

Russ nodded. "Okay, I think the *Blazers* made a good choice."

"I'm with you, Russ," Dad said, grinning at him.

I rolled my eyes.

Like my brother had any idea what he was talking about.

"How do you even know about Williams?" I asked.

Russ shrugged. "The sports section was mixed in with the newspaper pages I'm taking to my meeting tomorrow. I must have scanned a couple of articles without realizing it."

I rolled my eyes and shoved some popcorn in my mouth. I was better off focusing on the TV.

The Blazers were making some awesome plays, and even though it was a close and exciting game, Russ kept checking his watch. I finally asked, "Are you late for something?"

He sighed and tightened his grip on the book. "How can one quarter of a forty-eight-minute game possibly last more than twenty minutes?".

Math again?

"Time-outs and foul shots," I explained. "Are you even *watching*?"

"My point is that it doesn't add up," Russ said, reaching for the bowl. "The popcorn's good, though."

By halftime we were still up by seven, the Blazers were shooting 63 percent, and the popcorn was going fast.

In fact, it was gone when the third quarter started. And so was Russ.

"Don't worry," Dad said with a chuckle. "We'll make a basketball fan of him yet."

That's what I was afraid of.

RUSSELL

Weights and Measures

I woke up on Saturday morning and stared at my map of the solar system, which was always comforting. Earth was only *one* of all those planets and stars. And I was only *one* of billions of people on Earth. And of those billions, *millions* of people had bigger problems than basketball tryouts.

I couldn't help smiling.

I had a great book to read (a Blazer game had prevented me from enjoying it the night before), my Masters meeting was in a couple of hours, and tryouts would be nothing but a memory in less than a week.

I rolled out of bed and carried *Aidmere Lost* downstairs.

Of course, I wanted to pull things together for Masters of the Mind before I got lost in my book. As hard as it was to do it, I left the novel on the kitchen counter and found some of the items we needed for the challenge. Once I had the margarine container, aluminum foil, newspaper, and chopsticks from Jade Palace in a bag, I checked the fridge for eggs and heard Owen behind me.

"Milk, please," he said.

I handed him the jug and opened the egg carton to see what we had left. "Cool beans. Half a dozen."

"Just cool, Russ," he corrected. "Half a dozen what?"

"Eggs," I said, then told him about the challenge.

He rolled his eyes when I finished. "Why don't you guys ever build something people can use?"

"Like what?" I asked, wiping a smudge from my glasses.

"I don't know. Something that flies or whatever."

"Aircraft?" I asked, surprised. When he nodded, I went over our list of materials again. We couldn't exactly build a jet fighter out of chopsticks and newspapers. "This isn't Boeing," I told him. "It's Masters of the Mind."

He shrugged. "So, how about wrapping the eggs in rubber bands?"

"We'll only have six of them."

"But they're *rubber*. They'll help it bounce."

I shook my head. "It won't work."

He thought about it while a milk mustache dried on his upper lip. I was glad that he was interested enough to want to help, considering he'd never asked me a single question about Masters of the Mind before. Ever.

His interest got me thinking.

What if *Owen* joined the team as our fifth member? That would give the two of us something in common and add a very different point of view to the team.

I was just about to suggest it when he said, "Why don't you boil the egg? Water's on the list."

"Yes, but not boiling water," I reminded him.

"So heat it up." He shrugged.

"We don't have a heat source, Owen. Should we rub the chopsticks together to make fire?" I couldn't help laughing.

Owen glared at me like I'd hurt his feelings and left the room before I had a chance to say I was sorry.

Within seconds, I could hear a familiar noise: a basketball slamming against the pavement. Over and over.

Dad and Owen, at it again.

I didn't follow him outside because I was afraid they'd invite me to play. One wasted night in front of the TV was more than enough basketball for me, especially when I knew we'd be out practicing for tryouts in less than twenty-four hours.

I was already dreading it.

Once I'd read a few chapters and eaten a couple of blueberry muffins, Mom drove me and my shopping bag of challenge ingredients over to Nitu's house.

I hoped there would be some good news on the Chao replacement. I honestly couldn't understand why Masters of the Mind wasn't more popular with the rest of the kids at

Lewis and Clark. The competitions were fun, and so were all of the meetings and practices leading up to them. The team members were great, and they all loved problem solving, just like me.

Why did we have to *beg* people to join our team, when the Pioneers had to narrow players down through tryouts?

"So, basketball is a pretty interesting development," Mom said as she turned onto Nitu's street.

"*Interesting* is one word for it," I told her.

She glanced at me, looking worried. "You don't have to play, Russell."

"I won't," I said, laughing. "I'm not going to make the team."

She glanced at me, then back at the road. "You don't know that."

"Sure I do. And I'm fine with that. I don't have time to play basketball. And I don't even want to."

Mom pulled into Nitu's driveway. "Well, we're all proud of you, no matter what happens."

"I know, Mom." In my entire life, I'd never doubted that.

When I joined the rest of the team in Nitu's TV room, none of them were smiling.

Jason was the first to speak. "We have a problem."

I thought about our warm-up the other day. "Not enough time to find a squirrel rhyme?" I asked, chuckling as I dropped my backpack on the floor.

"No," Nitu said, grimly. "This is a curse that is much, much worse."

"At least double the trouble," Sara added.

"Is it something we can fix with some brainstorming tricks?" I asked.

"Can you guys stop rhyming, for, like, two seconds?" Jason asked.

"Sorry. What's wrong?"

"Only one person we've talked to wants to join the team," he said, quietly.

"Only one?" It was worse than I thought. But, as team leader, I didn't want them to know that. "Well, that's not the end of the world. I mean, one person is better than none, right?"

"You haven't heard who it is yet," Sara said with a sigh.

"Who is it?" I couldn't think of a single person we wouldn't want on the team.

That is, until Nitu moaned, "Arthur Richardson the Third."

I almost moaned myself.

Jason shrugged. "Yes, you heard, that turd the Third."

"Jason!" Sara gasped.

"What? I'm just rhyming."

"Maybe he'll bring new steam to the team," I said, hopefully.

"Will you make me scream in this bad dream?" Nitu asked.

Jason smiled. "Arthur takes 'creep' to a new extreme."

"I'm serious," I said. "Maybe he'll bring something new."

My teammates' jaws all dropped at the same time.

"Like a major headache?" Jason asked.

"No, like fresh ideas," I told him.

"You've got to be kidding," Nitu said, crossing her arms.

"He's smart," I reminded her.

"So he says," she replied.

Arthur's bragging *was* annoying. "Okay, well . . . he's willing to join us. And right now, that's half the battle."

"But, Russell," Nitu complained, "he's a total snob."

She was right about that, too. Arthur had transferred to Lewis and Clark from a private school in Connecticut at the beginning of the year. Most of the seventh grade had had their fill of him by the end of the first week.

The only topic he was interested in discussing was his plan to go to Harvard University. He carried a handkerchief in his pocket to wipe off cafeteria benches and classroom seats before he sat down. He wore cuff links to school.

Actually, I kind of liked the cuff links.

I'd tried talking to him in the beginning, and I'd even invited him to join my math study group. But he'd brushed me off.

I couldn't let my hurt feelings affect the Masters of the Mind team, though. "We need a teammate, Arthur wants to be one—"

"*Might* want to be one," Nitu corrected. "He'd like to come to a meeting to help him decide."

"Great," I said, hoping it would be a quick and painless decision for all of us. "And in the meantime, I think we need to get to work."

Our math whiz sighed with frustration, then shook her head, as though she was clearing it. "Okay, the team at Beaumont Middle School invited us to meet them for a friendly practice competition next Tuesday after school."

"That works for me," I said, and the rest of the group agreed.

"How did they do last year?" Jason asked. "I know they beat us at home, but how far did they go? Regionals?"

Nitu shook her head. "State."

"Seriously?" Jason gulped.

"And they came in second."

"Whoa," Jason said, quietly.

"So, we know they're good." I shrugged. "But I'd rather practice with a good team than a bad one, wouldn't you?"

"I guess so," he said, doubtfully.

"Hey, they're just like us, Jason."

"But better," he said, and sighed.

"Look," I said. "Let's get started, here. We should think about the egg challenge, since it needs the most preparation."

I started pulling items out of my backpack as Sara

marked each one off her checklist. Between the four of us, we had everything we needed, including duplicates of some items and even triplicates of duct tape and aluminum foil.

Sara and I got to work, sketching ideas onto our notepads. Jason and Nitu looked over each of the items on the table, trying to figure out which ones could be used together best and bouncing ideas back and forth.

I focused on trying to calculate how quickly the egg would be falling and how much of an impact would have to be absorbed by whatever we built.

It seemed like more than anything, we needed shocks.

Little did I know, there was a big one on the way.

Technical Foul

Mom called my bedroom a disaster zone, but it wasn't really that bad. The walls were covered with Blazers stuff, like last season's team poster, and a Camden jersey, hanging over my bed (the guy was still a Blazer to me, even if he *was* wearing a Jazz uniform that season). There was a Rip City Uprise flag on my desk. On my bulletin board I had ticket stubs from the games Dad took me to stuck next to a couple of programs.

It was pretty awesome.

I guess when Mom said disaster zone, she meant the clothes, games, and junk I'd dumped on the floor.

Oh, well.

After I finished beating Dad at HORSE, I changed into

my only clean pair of shorts and a gray Blazers T-shirt, then dug around to find my second-best pair of shoes. I was saving the brand-new ones for the Pioneers' season opener.

I was dressed in less than two minutes, which was probably a record, and out the door to meet the guys in three.

Man, I loved Saturday mornings.

Sunset Park was only a couple of blocks away, and I jogged there, figuring it couldn't hurt to warm up.

When I got to the park, Chris, Paul, Nate, and a couple of other guys were already waiting, so we had enough for three-on-three.

Awesome!

"No Nicky Chu?" I asked.

"It's his grandma's birthday," Paul said. "No Russ?" he asked, smiling like it was a joke.

"No, he has a . . ." I stopped because I knew they'd laugh if I said anything about Masters of the Mind. "He's helping my dad."

"Too bad," Nate said, laughing. "I'm dying to see his moves."

Paul snorted. "Yeah, I bet he's got some *killer* moves."

"Yeah, well, not today," I told them, kind of ticked off. "So, who's on my team?"

"Me," Chris said. "You, too, Nate?"

"Sure," he said, crossing the free-throw line to side with us.

"So, are we playing or what?" Paul asked, holding the ball.

"Oh, we're playing." Chris moved closer. "It's on, now."

"Oh yeah?" Paul asked. He started dribbling toward our net.

Chris was on him right away, so Paul passed to Mark, who came straight at me.

I kept my feet apart so I'd be ready to move in any direction, like Dad taught me. I bounced back and forth, hoping to steal the ball as soon as I got the chance.

The second Mark faked left, I snatched the ball and started dribbling toward their basket. I could hear him chasing me and Paul yelling for him to catch up, but I knew he wouldn't.

I dribbled in for a layup, smiling as the ball bounced off the backboard and right through the net.

"Sweet!" Nate said, giving me a high five.

Being on the court felt amazing. I loved the sound of the ball hitting the pavement; the guys shouting back and forth to pass, shoot, or block; and feeling like my lungs were on fire from running so hard.

After an hour, we all needed a break, so we flopped on the grass.

"Did you guys watch the game last night?" I asked, when I'd caught my breath. The Blazers had won by twelve points.

"It was awesome," Chris said.

"This might be our year," I told the guys. "The Blazers could be champs."

"So could the Pioneers," Paul said.

I smiled up at the sky. "Now *that* would be awesome."

"Yeah, but we'll have to make it through tryouts first," Chris groaned.

"No problem," Paul told him. "When Coach sees us rock the court, he'll put all of us on the team. Everything will be just like last year."

I couldn't wait.

I knew Dad was excited about Russell trying out, but I didn't know *how* excited until he woke us up on Sunday morning.

"Rise and shine, boys!" he shouted as he came up the stairs.

"What time is it?" I croaked when he tapped on my door.

"Time for a quick lap around the neighborhood before we get down to business."

Already?

I closed my eyes when I heard him go back downstairs, thinking I had a bit more time to lie there. But he swung my door wide open a few minutes later.

"Let's go, Owen. We're losing daylight."

Did we even *have* daylight yet?

By the time I'd dressed and double-knotted my Adidas, I could hear Russell moving around in his room.

I found Dad, some big glasses of milk, and a stack of toast in the kitchen.

He scooped some sugar into his coffee and sat down next to me. "Is Russ awake?"

Before I could answer, my brother was standing in the doorway. For a day of working out, he was wearing a green turtleneck and corduroy pants.

I looked at his feet.

Loafers.

"Hey, Russ," I said, taking a bite of my toast and waiting to see the look on Dad's face.

He looked up at my brother, then turned to stare at me.

All I could do was shrug.

Dad turned back to Russ. "You're going to need shorts."

"I thought it might be cold out there," Russ said.

"Not when we're *running*," I told him.

"Oh." He scratched his head and his hand disappeared in his curly hair. "Well, I don't have shorts, but I have some jeans or—"

"Owen," Dad interrupted, "maybe you can loan him some gear."

He hadn't noticed that Russ was built like a pencil and I was more of an eraser?

"I don't think my stuff will fit, Dad."

"Just give it a shot," he said.

I left my toast on my plate and led Russell upstairs.

Dad played basketball in college, and I knew he wanted me to follow in his footsteps, but did he really think Russ could, too?

There was no way.

In my closet, I found a T-shirt I'd almost grown out of and a pair of sweatpants I'd cut off into shorts. At least they had an elastic waistband.

While Russ got changed, I went into his room to find the cheap running shoes Mom bought when we were back-to-school shopping.

They were in his closet and still in the box, but not for the same reason that mine were. Mine were in mint condition for the season opener. But Russ's? I doubted he'd ever wear them outside of gym class.

I headed back to my room, where Russ was getting changed, and found some white socks in my top drawer.

When I turned around, my twin was standing in the middle of my room with his hands on his hips. It took only a second for me to guess that he was trying to hold up the shorts.

"Too big?" I asked, handing him the shoe box.

"No, these will work," he told me, but when he reached for the shoes, the shorts started falling down.

"I don't think so, Russ," I said, shaking my head. "Don't you have gym clothes?"

He shrugged. "They're at school."

"Of course." I sighed and went back to the closet to find my leather belt.

Man, if getting him dressed was this hard, how bad would the rest of it be?

When we got back to the kitchen, Dad gave me the look I remembered from when I tried to jump over our hedge on my bike but . . . didn't make it. And the hedge *really* didn't make it.

The look meant Dad wanted an explanation.

"We did our best," I told him, shrugging.

He squinted at Russ's shoes. "Where did you get those?"

"Sears," Russ told him. "Mom took us shopping before school started."

Dad looked at mine, which cost twice as much and looked about a thousand times better. "And where did yours come from?"

"Sears," I said, kind of embarrassed. "Last year. These are my old ones."

"Your *old* ones?" Dad asked, surprised.

"Yeah, I'm saving the new ones."

He looked at Russell's shoes again and shook his head. "I don't understand what your mom was thinking. Those don't look like they have any kind of ankle support."

"They were on sale," Russ explained. "I needed a scientific calculator."

"What?" Dad ran his fingers through his hair and stared at my brother.

I recognized that look, too. He was getting frustrated.

"A scientific calculator," Russ explained. "They're pretty expensive, so I got the cheaper shoes."

Dad turned to me. "I take it you didn't need a scientific calculator?"

Russ and I both cracked up at the same time.

Dad sighed and pointed us toward the table. "Okay, let's at least get you guys fed while I think."

I picked up my toast while Russell went straight for the milk.

"How about this?" Dad said, after a minute or so. "Owen, you can lend Russ your new shoes for today and—"

"What?" I gasped. My brand-new-mint-condition-still-in-the-box-and-saved-for-the-past-month shoes?

"They won't fit," Russ said, stopping my panic attack. "We haven't had the same size feet since we were babies, Dad."

Dad sighed. "Okay, then we use a backup plan."

"What backup plan?" I asked, hoping it didn't have anything to do with wrecking *my* stuff.

"We'll head down to the mall this morning and get Russ some gear. He's going to need shoes, shorts . . . and anything else, Russ?"

What?

Mom always split the back-to-school shopping right

down the middle, and now Russ was going to get a bunch of new stuff?

Russ shook his head, looking worried. "Dad, I don't think I need—"

"Of course you do," Dad said. "You can't play basketball in that . . . outfit."

He had to be kidding!

New gear would be worn once or twice, *max*, then dumped in the back of his closet, forever.

What a total waste!

Seriously, buying a third pair of shoes for me would be a better investment. And I even knew which ones I wanted.

"He's only trying out," I reminded Dad.

"Exactly." Russell nodded. "It would be a waste of money to—"

"It's not a waste of anything," Dad said, reaching over to pat his shoulder. "These are basic necessities if you're going to play ball this year."

"But I'm not," Russ told him. "I'm not going to make the team, Dad."

"You don't know that," he said. "Coach wants you to try out for a reason."

"I know. One reason: I'm tall."

"It's *basketball*, son. Being tall is half the battle."

Russell slumped in his chair and didn't say anything else.

It was kind of weird to see someone look that sad about

getting new shoes and shorts. Then again, I probably would have had a total meltdown if anyone tried to give me a scientific calculator.

"Let's finish up with breakfast, get your gear, and we can start training," Dad said, taking the last gulp of his coffee.

Yeah, right. *Training*.

The Conversion Factor

It turned out that my Sunday morning wasn't eaten up by the dreaded basketball training. It was much worse than that. The hours were devoured by . . . shopping.

"So, how was yesterday's meeting?" Dad asked during the drive to the mall.

Just like Owen, he'd never asked me about Masters of the Mind before. Ever.

"It was fine."

"You boys are ready for the big game?" he asked.

"District competition," I corrected. "And it's a mixed team. Boys and girls."

"Oh, sure," Dad said. "A mixed team. So, what are you working on?"

I described the oral quiz and the egg-drop challenge.

"Two stories, huh?" Dad asked. "Can you boil the water?"

"Ha!" Owen turned and grinned at me. "That's what *I* asked."

"We have no heat source," I told him.

"Gotcha." Dad nodded. "So you'll drop the egg out of the window, and if it breaks . . . ?"

"Even if it cracks, we'll be eliminated."

"And if you win?" he asked.

"We go to Regionals, then State, then the National Championship."

"Like basketball," Owen said.

Not like basketball at all, actually. We were creative problem solving, not throwing a ball around.

"Huh," Dad said, but didn't ask anything else.

Why couldn't my family give Masters of the Mind a chance?

The van was quiet for a couple of minutes, and I realized it was up to me to keep the conversation going.

"Arthur Richardson the Third wants to join the team," I said, knowing he was in at least one of Owen's classes.

"Arthur the what?" Dad asked, chuckling. "He sounds like a medieval knight."

"No, he's a geek," Owen said.

I wondered if my brother knew how many times *I'd* been called a geek.

"He's fine," I said, even though I doubted it was true. "He's smart and we need another team member."

"Why didn't you ask me?" Owen asked.

What? "Well, I didn't think you—"

"I'm *kidding*, Russ," he said, and laughed.

"You are?"

"Duh. Like I'm gonna be a mathlete and you're gonna play basketball. Ha!"

I smiled back at him, relieved.

"Hey, don't count Russ out," Dad said, winking at me in the mirror.

But counting me out was exactly what I wanted them to do.

When we got to the mall, I followed Owen and Dad past several perfectly good stores and into one called Go Time. It was packed with clothing, equipment, and employees dressed in team uniforms, grinning at us like old friends.

I'd shopped with Mom enough to know that salespeople were on commission, and the best deals were on the clearance rack. I started to head in that direction, but it turned out that Dad didn't care about saving money.

In fact, when a salesman approached him and said that he had the perfect pair of shoes for me, Dad was happy to follow him to an enormous Nike display.

"I don't need Nikes," I said, but no one was listening.

Whenever I felt frustrated or nervous, I calmed down by working my way through the periodic table of elements.

Beryllium, boron, carbon, nitrogen.

I glanced around the store, looking for some kind of a knockoff brand, but Go Time seemed to sell only the big names.

I watched Dad listening to the salesman, as if the shoes I wore for a single afternoon really mattered. And that's when I knew that the tryout situation was officially out of control.

All I wanted to do was go home and be the Russell Evans I'd been for my entire life.

The brain.

Oxygen, fluorine, neon, sodium.

I didn't want all the extra complications.

Magnesium, aluminum, silicon.

I didn't want a special outfit for *not* making the team. But as I took a deep breath, getting ready to tell Dad how I felt, I saw it in the salesman's hand.

It was dark blue, with an even darker sole. The pattern looked like a drafting blueprint, and the silver *swoosh* stitched on the side practically screamed "speed."

He put the shoe in my hand so I could see if I liked it, but he was too late.

I was already in love.

And that was only the beginning.

The athletic socks Dad chose felt like pillows wrapped around my feet. And as soon as I tried them on with my new Nikes, I was ready to throw out every black and brown pair in my sock drawer at home. Dad found two pairs of shorts for me, one blue and the other silver, which matched those amazing shoes perfectly.

It was funny; I'd never cared about my clothes matching before.

I'd never cared about the logo on a T-shirt or the fit of a track jacket either, until I stood in the dressing room at Go Time, looking at the complete stranger in the mirror.

Of course, it was still me, but a new and improved me. A cooler me.

In fact, I looked *so* cool, I actually started to feel excited about tryouts.

What if I made the team?

I could wear the new clothes all the time.

I looked at the Nikes.

What if I made the team?

If I was a Pioneer, Owen and I would have more in common than ever before. Maybe I'd start to enjoy the endless basketball talk at the dining room table. I might even become a Blazers fan.

What if I made the team?

I'd never even considered the positive side of trying out.

Could my brother and I play with each other? Could me and my twin manage to win?

I never dreamed I'd be rhyming about basketball, so I couldn't help smiling.

When Dad was satisfied that I had everything I needed, we piled my mountain of bags into the car to drive home. All the way there, I thought about how different my life would be if I became a Pioneer.

Of course, there was nothing wrong with my life. It was great.

But it could be even better.

When we got to the house, Mom looked annoyed when we unloaded all the bags from the trunk.

My excitement started to fade.

The noble gases: helium, neon, argon, krypton, xenon, and radon.

"Did you have a good time?" she asked, her voice sounding a bit tight in her throat.

"Yes," I said. "Thanks for the new gear, Mom."

"You're welcome," she said, looking at Dad with a raised eyebrow, then following us inside.

While I was climbing the stairs to put my things away, I overheard my parents talking.

"Well, I guess he needed some bits and pieces," Mom said.

"Definitely, and we got him some great gear, Susan. You should have seen how excited he was when he saw those shoes."

"Good," she said, but her tone didn't sound like she meant it. "It's just . . . a lot of stuff. A lot of . . . expense."

"I know, but I felt like I needed to do it for Russ."

"For *Russ*, huh?" she asked, doubtfully.

I knew what she meant. I'd seen how much fun Dad had shopping at Go Time.

"Look," Dad said, "he's never shown the slightest bit of interest in sports."

"That's my point," Mom said.

"I'm not forcing him into anything."

"I didn't say you were." She sighed. "I just don't want this to be a repeat of the football disaster or that mess with baseball, you know?"

I cringed at the memory.

"I know, but with this opportunity falling into his lap, I can't help wanting him to try. Sports are an important part of being a kid. He needs to *be* a kid."

What?

"What do you mean by that?" Mom asked.

"Honey, just . . . look at him next to Owen."

"Owen's different."

Cesium, francium . . .

"No, Susan. *Russell* is the one who's different."

I didn't want to hear another word, so I quickly ran into my bedroom to change my clothes. In less than a minute, I sneaked past the kitchen and out the front door.

The excitement I'd felt about my new gear and being part of the team had vanished.

How disappointed would Dad be when I had to tell him I'd failed at tryouts? Wasn't there some other way I could show him I was "normal"?

I looked down at my Nikes.

Would I have to leave all the new clothes in my closet if I didn't make the Pioneers?

I knew the answer to that already.

Medical students who failed their final exam didn't hang stethoscopes around their necks. People kicked out of the space program didn't wear jet packs when they went grocery shopping.

I tried to think positive thoughts, but there was so much clogging my brain, I couldn't come up with any.

Owen had always said that exercise cleared his head, and I hoped it could do the same thing for me. So, for the first time in my life, I was looking forward to running.

That is, until we actually *started* running.

Of course, my brain knew that I was too young for a heart attack, but my legs didn't. Neither did my aching lungs. Or my throbbing feet. Even my hair hurt.

And that was only the first block.

But as we ran, Owen encouraged me. He told me how to breathe properly and to hold my arms steady, instead of letting them wave around like the wind socks at Grandma's. He stayed with me for every step, matching my pace and trying to help me reach our destination in one piece.

It helped, but not enough.

Then, when I was sure I was seconds away from collapsing, I glanced down at those new Nikes. Even though I felt the worst I ever had, I felt a smile creep onto my face.

I was still panting and cramping up, but I'd found something positive.

When I looked down at those Nikes, I forgot about what Dad had said.

I felt like a real athlete.

I don't know what it was about that shiny blue and silver fabric, but I knew those shoes were as magical as Superman's cape or Spider-Man's skintight suit.

They made me feel like I could do anything.

Maybe even play basketball.

Bounce Pass

When I saw how upset Russ looked when Mom and Dad were talking about him, I kind of stopped caring that he got all that cool new gear or that Dad wanted to turn him into a Blazers fan.

Actually, that's not true. I didn't stop *caring* about the gear, because it was so awesome I wanted it all for myself. But Russ needed my help *more* than I needed another pair of sneakers.

After all, a pair of shoes wasn't going to make him normal by Wednesday, no matter how cool they were. Without my help, he was going to be a total disaster at tryouts. And even though it stunk like old cheese that I'd have to use up my Sunday helping him, I knew he'd always helped me out when I'd needed it.

I thought about all the times he'd explained math assignments that made no sense. Then there was my fifth-grade science project, when I mixed up my bug types and labeled them all wrong on my poster. Russ had stayed up late, helping me fix it, even though he had an English essay due the next day.

Russ always looked out for me, and it was my turn to look out for him (even if it was mostly so he wouldn't embarrass me).

I did my best to be positive and cheer him on while we ran, and with my help he actually made it to Sunset Park.

Barely, but he made it.

I reached over to untuck his T-shirt.

Nobody tucks T-shirts into basketball shorts.

"Okay, now let's get you playing as good as you look," I said.

Russell sighed. "I doubt that's going to happen."

"Hey," I said, punching his shoulder. "You don't look *that* good."

Russ laughed. "Very funny."

"Let's do this," Dad said after he'd caught his breath.

All three of us were hot, sweaty, and super tired.

But that was basketball.

"The court's bigger than I thought," Russ said, looking from one basket to the other.

"It's the same as the gym at school," I told him. "After you run back and forth a hundred times, you won't even notice it."

"Right," he said. "I can barely run a block, Owen."

"Well, you just ran a bunch of them." Kind of. By the end it was more limping than jogging.

He didn't say anything, but slowly nodded as he walked onto the court.

"Okay, Russ," Dad said. "Let's start nice and slow. I want you to just dribble toward me."

I tossed my brother the ball.

He missed it, and it rolled down the grass hill.

"I'll get it," I said.

When I came back with the ball, he whispered, "Sorry. And thanks."

"Okay, let's try again. Toward me," Dad said, from under the hoop.

Dribbling the ball twenty feet seemed like the easiest thing ever, but not for Russ. He bounced the ball a couple of times, then held it while he took two steps, then stopped and bounced it again.

A group of teenagers hanging out on the picnic benches watched, and one of them said, "Uh . . . traveling?"

"And double dribbling," another guy chipped in.

I felt my face get hot.

Come on, Russ.

"Dribble a little faster," Dad said. "And try to do it while you're walking. Aim for a bounce or two with each step."

"And bounce it harder, too," I told him. "So you don't have to bend so much."

I heard more laughing from the picnic tables when Russ tried again.

"Okay, the ball isn't going to hurt you, Russ," Dad explained, rubbing his forehead.

My brother gritted his teeth and bounced it hard. It hit one of his new shoes and flew off down the hill again.

Great.

When I went after it, I thought about how weird it was that Dad and I thought basketball was fun and Russ thought it was torture.

Even when we were little, he didn't like normal stuff. When I went nuts over my first regulation-size basketball one Christmas, Russ messed around with the ball pump all day, taking it apart and putting it back together again, like a puzzle.

While I played with a robot from Grandpa, Russ stared at the weird little drawings that came with it. "Schematics," he called them. I'm pretty sure he made that word up.

"Just relax," I heard Dad tell Russ as I climbed back up the hill. "Remember, it's only a game."

But it wasn't only a game for Russell anymore. And how was he supposed to relax after Dad said he wasn't normal?

He had to be ready on Wednesday, or I'd never hear the end of it from the guys.

But he was already way worse at basketball than I'd imagined.

And he hadn't even taken a shot yet.

It turned out to be the longest day ever.

Dad spent three hours trying to be patient with the most uncoordinated kid on the planet.

I ran up and down the hill to retrieve the ball about six thousand times.

And Russ spent the whole afternoon trying to get even *one* of the things we were teaching him, and blowing it.

When he wasn't dropping the ball, he was bending over to retie his shoelaces.

"Maybe you should try double knots," I suggested, when I couldn't take it anymore.

"I'll never get them undone," Russ said, with a shrug.

"Russ." I groaned. "That's the whole idea."

"Come on, boys," Dad called from down the court. "Let's keep it moving."

When we were ready to go home and Dad pushed us to stay another half hour, I thought he was crazy. But it turned out he was right.

By that time, we knew for a fact that Russ was slow and his ball handling was garbage. On the plus side, we knew that he got tired really fast, but he could push through the cramps and keep going most of the time.

But in those last thirty minutes, we learned something even more important.

Russ and I stood under the basket, watching Dad come in for a shot. Without anyone telling him what to do, Russ lifted his hands and blocked it.

"Nice move!" Dad said, thumping him on the back and passing me the ball. "Let's try it again. Owen?"

I went in from the other side and when I aimed, Russ knocked the ball loose and it hit the pavement behind me.

"Denied!" Dad shouted, totally excited.

I couldn't believe what I was seeing.

We took a bunch more shots, and Russ stopped almost half of them.

"Whew!" Dad said, wiping his forehead with the sleeve of his T-shirt. "Nice work. Let's call it a day."

On the walk home, I told Russ I was impressed with how hard he'd tried, and how he hadn't given up.

"Thanks, but I'm still pretty nervous about this, Owen," he said quietly.

So was I. Sure, it had been cool to see Russ kind of start to get the hang of basketball, but trying hard wasn't exactly the same as being good.

And that's when an awesome idea hit me. An idea that could save us both at tryouts. "Look, we know you're not the best player."

"Thanks a lot."

"You know what I mean. But that doesn't matter."

"It doesn't?" he asked, surprised.

"No, you've got something the other guys don't."

"A sixth-grade math trophy?"

"No. Well, yeah, but something better."

He looked at me like that was impossible.

I smiled. "You're tall and you can block a lot of shots."

"So?"

"*So?*" I laughed. "So all you have to do on Wednesday is stand there and wave your arms."

It was genius. He wouldn't embarrass himself (or me!) and tryouts would be quick and painless.

I watched Russ limping next to me.

Well, maybe not painless.

Still, the plan was pretty brilliant.

"Just stand there?" he asked, looking at me like I was nuts.

I nodded and grinned. "Just stand there."

RUSSELL

Negative Impact

Our next Masters of the Mind practice was on Tuesday, followed immediately by a practice session with the Beaumont Middle School team.

When I got to Jason's house, his dad was watching a Blazers game in the living room.

"How is DeShawn Williams playing, Mr. Schmidt?" I asked.

His head whipped around so fast, I thought it might come right off his neck. "Fantastic," he said, grinning. "He's hit every free throw."

"He's shooting seventy-four percent for the season so far," I told him, remembering the statistic I'd seen in our morning newspaper. It was kind of strange that what would have been a C grade in school was headline news in basketball.

"Do you want to watch?" he asked, hopefully. "I've got three kids in this house and no one likes basketball."

"Thanks, but I should get to the meeting."

"Masters of the Mind," he said, with a big sigh.

He sounded just like my dad.

When I opened Jason's bedroom door, everyone was sitting on the floor, squeezed between his bed, his tuba, and a prize-winning Lego battleship.

It wasn't the perfect arrangement, but it would work.

As soon as I sat down, I saw Jason staring at my new Nikes, and I felt proud of how cool they were. In fact, I was so busy admiring them that it took me a minute to notice the gloom in the room.

"What's going on?" I asked.

Before anyone could answer, the bedroom door swung open.

There stood Arthur Richardson the Third, dressed in brand-new khakis and a red golf shirt embroidered with a Harvard emblem. His blond hair was parted so perfectly that I wondered if he'd done it with a ruler instead of a comb.

"Hey, Arthur," Jason said.

Arthur looked down his nose at all of us (which isn't really as bad as it sounds because our faces were at his knee level).

"We're sitting on the floor?" he asked. His eyes were wide, like he couldn't believe what he was seeing.

"Uh, yes," Jason said, glancing at Sara, who shrugged.

Arthur Richardson the Third sighed and sat down next to me.

"I'm Russell," I said, reaching to shake his hand.

He ignored it. "I know."

"I'm Nitu," our math whiz said, with a smile.

"I know that," Arthur said, impatiently. "I know who all of you *are*."

There was a moment of awkward silence.

"So . . . welcome to the team," Sara said, quietly.

Arthur raised one eyebrow in her direction. "I haven't committed yet," he said. "I'll make my decision after the meeting."

Since I was the one who'd pushed the rest of the team to give him a chance, I tried to smooth things over. "Sure," I said, nodding slowly, "you're trying out for us and—"

Arthur looked at me like I'd told him the square root of sixteen was seven. "No," he said. "*You're* trying out for me."

Nitu, Jason, Sara, and I exchanged a look.

I cleared my throat. "Well, we're glad to have you here today, to uh, *consider* joining our team. Masters of the Mind is great way to—"

"Have you ever won Nationals?" he interrupted.

I took a breath. "No."

He sniffed. "State?"

I glanced at Nitu, who was scowling at him. "No," I admitted.

"Regionals?"

I cleared my throat. "We're a fairly new team and—"

"A yes or no is all I need," he said.

"Then no," I answered, feeling my entire body tensing.

Alkaline earth metals: beryllium, magnesium, calcium.

"I see," he said. "So, you'd like me to join a losing team."

"No, we wouldn't," Nitu said, and I turned to see a dangerous look in her eyes.

I quickly jumped in. "What Nitu means is that we don't want you to join a losing team. We want you to join a team with the *potential* to win."

"We can take the heat when it's time to compete," Jason said, cracking a smile.

"When we get a high score, we work for more," Sara added.

"If we—" Nitu began.

"What are you doing?" Arthur interrupted, frowning.

"Uh," Jason said, glancing at me before explaining, "sometimes we rhyme."

"*Sometimes you rhyme?*" Arthur looked disgusted, like he'd just been told we pick each other's noses.

"It's like a warm-up," Sara said, looking embarrassed.

"Okay," I said, ready to move on before Arthur ruined

the whole meeting. "I've been thinking about this egg challenge and—"

"We have a problem," Nitu said.

It seemed like we had a lot more than one.

Strontium, barium, radium.

"What is it?" I asked.

No one said a word as I looked from one face to the next, waiting.

Finally, Sara spoke. "The school will only pay half of our entry fee for the district competition."

I was stunned. "What do you mean?"

"Just what she said," Jason told me. "We have to pay the other half ourselves. By *Monday*."

"That can't be right," I told the group.

"It's right," Jason said. "I mean, it's *wrong*, but it's right. We're doomed."

"Half the entry fee?" I asked again.

Sara nodded. "Nitu and I talked to Mr. Wills this afternoon, and those are the rules."

"And we don't have the money." Nitu sighed.

"Let me get this straight," Arthur interrupted. "You want me to join a losing team with no budget?"

"Not really," Nitu said, shooting him another look.

"Listen, Art. We—" I began.

"Arthur," he corrected.

"Okay, Arthur. This team is—"

"Lucky I came along," he interrupted. "Not only was I

the top student at Connecticut's Walter Borderton Preparatory School, but my family is . . ." He paused and looked down at his hands, as though he was embarrassed, but we all knew he wasn't. ". . . very wealthy."

"How nice for you," Nitu said through gritted teeth.

"I'll have my father write a check."

"No, thank you," I told him.

"Why not?" He pointed at Sara. "She already said you don't have the money."

I took a deep breath. "It's our responsibility to raise the money," I said, relieved when the rest of the group nodded. "So we're lucky that this is a problem-solving club and—"

"Don't be stupid," Arthur interrupted. "My father can just—"

Stupid?

"I'm team leader, Arthur, and I'm calling a vote."

It took about two seconds for three hands to fly into the air and reject the idea of Arthur's father paying our registration fees.

Arthur sulked while the rest of us tried to come up with a real solution.

"What about a fund-raiser?" Nitu suggested.

"What kind of a fund-raiser?" Jason asked, and the brainstorming began.

The meeting had already exhausted me, and it had barely started.

As the minutes passed, I liked Arthur a little bit less every time he opened his mouth. And that was often.

Eventually, I did something I'd never done at a Masters meeting before. I started daydreaming about something else.

And even more surprising?

That something else was basketball.

When we finished up at Jason's house, we walked over to the public library on Northwest Thurman to meet the Beaumont team. They had a great track record, but we weren't going to let that bother us.

However, it looked like we might be in trouble when Beaumont's team of five filed into the library wearing matching T-shirts and serious expressions. They each carried a black briefcase, embroidered with the Masters of the Mind logo.

Uh-oh.

Halogens: fluorine, chlorine, bromine and astatine.

The team leader, Peter, introduced himself.

"Hi, I'm Russ," I told him, gripping his hand firmly.

"Russell Evans," he said, with a quick nod. "Winner of the sixth-grade math award. Consistent appearances on the Lewis and Clark Middle School honor roll."

"Whoa," Jason whispered.

"Jason Schmidt," Peter continued, without being introduced. "Second-place finish in last year's district Science Fair for a project on lunar landings."

"Uh, yeah," Jason said.

Peter worked his way through Sara and Nitu's achievements, then stared at Arthur. "You're not in my file."

He had a file?

"Arthur Richardson the Third," Arthur said, ignoring Peter's offer of a handshake.

Peter pointed to his teammates and very quickly said, "Emma, Jorge, and the Digby twins."

"Oh, I'm a twin, too, but—" I started to tell him.

"We know," Peter said.

Was there anything they *didn't* know?

"Okay," I said, trying to regain some control. "We thought we could start with—"

"I printed meeting agendas for everyone," Peter said, taking a seat at the head of the table. The rest of his team surrounded him, none of them saying a word.

I signaled to my team to sit as well. They all looked as nervous as I was. Except for Arthur, anyway. He looked like he smelled something he didn't like.

But he always looked like that.

For the next two hours, Beaumont put us to the test.

And believe it or not, we passed.

Nitu, Sara, and Jason put their brains in high gear, going

toe-to-toe with the competition while Arthur Richardson the Third went a step further. He dominated our practice session with fast, smart answers and didn't make a single mistake.

The truth was, everyone shone but me.

I just couldn't wrap my head around even the simplest problems. And when I did give an answer, it wasn't a very good one.

For the first time since I'd joined Masters of the Mind, I was struggling.

And I didn't like it.

Free Throw

My alarm clock went off on Wednesday morning, and I could think of only one thing.

Tryout day!

I stared at the ceiling, imagining running drills and seeing my name on the team list. I was sure I'd make the roster, but my stomach felt weird, like there were jumping beans in there.

I had a shower and grabbed the Adidas box from my closet. I'd been planning to save the shoes for the Pioneers' first game, but having an edge at tryouts wouldn't hurt. I took off the lid, pulled the tissue paper out of the way and smiled.

Mint condition!

They were dark blue with white stripes and light-blue stitches. It had been hard to choose between them and a red pair, but I'd decided I wanted my shoes to match my Pioneers uniform.

Just like Russ.

I lifted one shoe out of the box for a closer look. When I first saw them, I'd thought they were the coolest shoes on the planet. But that was before I saw my brother's. I stared at the Adidases and realized they weren't half as cool as his Nikes.

I closed the box and shoved it into my backpack, trying not to think about it. I was supposed to be supporting Russ, just like he supported me. It wasn't about shoes. Or T-shirts. Or those awesome shorts with the stripes down the sides that he got two pairs of. Or the sweet hoodie I wished was hanging in *my* closet.

It was about making sure Russ didn't embarrass me (or himself, of course) at tryouts. Period.

And besides, I could forget about the gear because Russell's basketball career was going to be over in like, seconds. All he'd have left after tryouts were the shoes.

The Nikes would be souvenirs, like the "parting gifts" they gave to people who lost on game shows.

"Big day," Mom said as I walked into the kitchen. "I made waffles."

"Awesome," I told her, even though they were *Russ's* favorite, not mine.

"Any sign of your brother?" she asked.

"I think he's in the shower," I told her through a mouthful.

"I hope he does well today," Mom said quietly. "I know your dad gave him a pep talk last night, but—"

"He'll be fine." All he had to do was stand there. He could do that. Even the maple tree in our front yard could do that. In fact, it *did*. Like, twenty-four seven.

When I left the house, Chris was waiting for me on the corner with a ball under his arm.

"Finally," he said when I caught up with him. "Are you ready?"

"Yup. I've even got brand-new shoes." I pointed toward my pack.

"Cool. I'm wearing my lucky underwear."

If it was the same underwear he'd worn all the way through last year's semifinals, they weren't lucky.

In fact, I felt sorry for them.

"I've been working on my jump shot," he said when we were about halfway to school.

What?

"You have a jump shot?" The jumping beans in my stomach started moving.

I didn't have a jump shot!

"I haven't mastered it yet," Chris said. "But my brother said seventh grade is when coaches want to see what you can do from the field." He shrugged. "You know, three-pointers."

What? No one told me that!

"But last year was free throws and layups," I reminded him. "And staying close to the hoop."

"That was last year." Chris shrugged again. "My brother said the school record is thirteen three-pointers in seventh grade."

"Are you kidding me?"

I'd never scored a three-pointer in my whole life! Sure, I'd been close, but like my grandpa always said, close only counted in horseshoes and hand grenades, whatever that meant.

Would Coach Baxter really be expecting us to make jump shots?

Would I be able to do one under pressure?

Could I do one *at all*?

I doubted it.

I made it through my morning classes, and during lunch me, Chris, Nate, Paul, and Nicky sat together to trade snacks and talk about what was going to happen that afternoon.

"Did you say jump shot?" Nicky asked Chris.

"Uh-huh." Chris grunted, biting into Paul's apple.

"No one said anything to me about jump shots," Nicky muttered.

"Tell me about it." I groaned, glad I wasn't the only one who couldn't do them.

"I can only make maybe two out of five," Nicky said, and sighed.

"What?" I practically choked. Maybe I *was* the only one, after all.

"I can only hit a three-pointer in about one out of *ten* shots," Paul said.

That made me feel a little better.

But only until Nate said, "Dude, this is tryout day! You've gotta do better than that."

I tried to drown my jumping beans with a juice box, but they seemed to know how to swim.

After lunch, I was on my way to social studies and trying not to freak out when I overheard Russ and some other kids in the hallway.

"Man, those shoes are awesome!" Ryan McNichol told him.

What?

I forgot all about jump shots and three-pointers. Russ was wearing his brand-new shoes? To school? Sure, he'd worn them to practice at Sunset Park, but to *school*?

He wasn't saving them for the gym floor?

I shook my head. Of course he wasn't.

I mean, saving them for what? He wasn't going to make the team, so why not wear them every day? Why not mess up the most awesome shoes on the planet without even thinking about it? What difference did it make?

"Thanks," Russ said. "My dad got them for me."

"I heard you're trying out for basketball," Jeff Billings said.

I peeked around the corner. Russ looked way more comfortable than I would have expected, considering it was a conversation about sports, not space stations.

"Yeah. I know I won't make it, but Coach Baxter wants me to try."

"You never know," Jeff said. "You're pretty tall, and they could probably use a tall guy."

With skills, I wanted to shout. Tall or not, a guy still had to be able to dribble! They made it sound like anyone could do it!

"You're really trying out?" Maria asked. "That's so cool. Good luck, Russell."

"Thanks, I'll need it," he said, laughing.

I walked over to his locker when the other kids left. "Want to take some practice shots at afternoon break?" I asked.

"Thanks, Owen, but I'm too busy," he said.

"Tryouts are *today*," I reminded him. "Like, in a couple of hours."

He pushed up his glasses and squinted at me. "I think we've gone over this. I'm not going to make the team, Owen."

"I know," I said, nodding. "But we want to make sure you do okay."

"We practiced on the weekend," he said. "You told me to just stand there."

"I know, but—"

"You said that would be enough." He was starting to look worried.

"Sure, but—"

"You think I'm doomed?" he asked, sounding just like that Jason kid on his brainiac team.

"Okay, never mind the practice," I told him. "Do you think you'll be able to block the shots the way you did at Sunset Park?"

He held his books tight against his bony chest. "I think so."

"Then you're cool. All you have to do is show up, stand there, and when it's over, you'll never have to worry about basketball again."

At least that's what I thought.

The Intersection of Sets

When I met the Masters team during afternoon break, I was in bad shape. Any ideas I'd had about surviving tryouts had been destroyed by Owen.

And, more importantly, my confidence in my Masters skills had been seriously damaged during the practice session with Beaumont. I'd been useless.

But then I found out I had even more to worry about.

"We have a problem," Sara said.

"Another one?" I asked. "Maybe our fund-raiser should be selling 'We have a problem' T-shirts."

"Very funny," Nitu said. "But we do need to talk about the fund-raiser."

"Okay, let's meet tomorrow, at our usual—"

"It's my dad's birthday tomorrow," Nitu interrupted. "Remember? We rescheduled our regular meeting for today."

"Yeah, and we have to figure out the fund-raising *today*," Jason said, nodding. "We talked to Mr. Wills this morning, and if we're going to set up any kind of a booth at school, we need to give forty-eight hours' notice."

Forty-eight hours? That *was* a problem. The registration had to be paid by Monday!

"But they didn't give us any notice that they wouldn't pay the whole fee," I reasoned.

"Russell," our math whiz said, resting a hand on my arm. "They don't care."

"Okay," I said, trying to think of an alternative. "Let's not have the fund-raiser at school."

"Where else are we going to do it?" Nitu asked, hands on her hips.

It was my turn to shrug. "We don't even know what 'it' is, yet."

"Which is why we all need to meet after school *today*," Jason said. "We have to get this figured out."

"You guys know I have basketball tryouts."

Jason took another look at my Nikes, and this time he didn't look impressed at all.

"Russell," Nitu said, shaking her head. "Don't you see how important this is?"

"Of course I do," I told her. "Obviously, it's more

important to me than the tryouts, but there's nothing I can do. I was told to be there."

"What are we supposed to do?" Sara asked.

"Have the meeting without me," I told them. "Just like we planned."

"Without you, but *with* Arthur?" Nitu asked, raising an eyebrow.

"Has he told anyone whether he's joining the team?" I asked, dreading the answer.

They all shook their heads.

"Well, if he wants to, we can't leave him out of the meetings." Which was too bad. "And who knows? He might have come up with some great ideas."

"Like having his father pay off the principal so he won't demand forty-eight hours' notice?" Jason asked, rolling his eyes.

"Very funny," I said. "Look, Arthur was probably just being difficult about the money yesterday because the team is new to him and he doesn't know where he's going to fit in with us."

"*If* he commits to joining," Nitu said, offering another eye roll.

"Yes, if he commits." I sighed, half hoping he wouldn't. Things were complicated enough without him. "And if he does, we welcome a new brain. Agreed?" I looked at each of them in turn, and they all quietly nodded.

The bell rang and we said our good-byes.

"Sara, can you call me tonight and fill me in on the meeting?" I asked, just as she was leaving. She was the most likely to give me a fair update.

"I will." She nodded. "And Russell?"

"Yes?"

"Good luck at tryouts," she said with a shy smile.

"Thank you."

I couldn't concentrate in any of my classes. There was way too much going on in every part of my life, and tryouts were the least of it. I'd lost my Masters of the Mind confidence, I had no idea how to keep Arthur off the team, how to raise the money for our registration, or how to drop an egg from two stories without breaking it.

What kind of a leader was I?

A well-dressed one, apparently. I'd been complimented all day on my new shoes, and I couldn't believe how much impact a bit of rubber and nylon had on my popularity. Of course, it was an incredibly cool blend of rubber and nylon, but still. Those shoes got me more attention than my honor roll appearances or my perfect score on the sixth-grade math exam.

Suddenly, I had a new understanding of why some girls

spent so much time fixing their hair and comparing outfits, and some boys cared so much about wearing the right jeans.

$$\times \quad \div \quad +$$

When the final bell rang, I took a deep breath and gathered my new sports gear from my locker. It was a shame to think it would only be worn once, but there was nothing I could do about that.

As I walked down the hallway, I hoped the Masters would have a good meeting without me. And "good" meant no Arthur.

If he was out of the way, I was fairly sure I could get back on track. The more I thought about it, the more certain I was that the distractions of Arthur and tryouts were what had thrown me off my Masters game. I wasn't losing my skills, I was just . . . sidetracked.

When I walked into the boys' locker room, the buzz of conversation I'd heard from the hallway suddenly stopped.

I froze, unsure of what to do.

A week ago, I wouldn't have dreamed I'd be standing in a locker room about to try out for the basketball team. A week ago, all I'd been worried about was Chao moving to Cincinnati and whether we'd make it through a single competition without him.

Life had been so much easier when all I had to think

about were Masters of the Mind and Math Club. But I'd wasted study time practicing for the basketball court and classroom time worrying about whether I'd be good enough.

Of course I wouldn't.

And everyone knew it.

Even when I'd been excited about what it would feel like to be a Pioneer, I'd known it would never happen.

Owen was the jock. I was the brains. And that was how it was supposed to be.

I cleared my throat and looked at the guys.

The room was dead silent, and everyone was staring at me like I didn't belong.

And they were right. I didn't.

I belonged at a table with my Masters of the Mind friends, not standing alone while a crowd of jocks I barely knew looked me over from head to toe, wondering what I was doing there.

What was I doing there?

Every cell in my body told me that I was making a big mistake. That I was about to humiliate myself in front of a live audience.

The nitrogen group: nitrogen, phosphorus, arsenic, antimony, and bismuth.

"Seriously?" Paul asked, staring at me from his spot on the bench. "You're seriously trying out?"

"Yes," I said, quietly.

Owen's friends kept staring at me. I waited for someone, anyone, to say something, but nobody did.

I couldn't think of a time when I'd felt more out of place. *More wrong.*

I took a deep breath, realizing that talking about trying out and actually doing it were two very different things. These jocks would be watching every move I made, then laughing about it for weeks.

I glanced at my Nikes.

What had I been thinking?

A pair of shoes wouldn't save me.

I needed to just turn around and walk away. I'd be better off going to the Masters meeting and helping my team than embarrassing myself because a new coach came up with a terrible idea.

But just as I was about to leave, I heard Owen's voice.

Turnover

"Come here," I said, waving Russ over to an empty spot on the bench.

He looked like he had a panic button in his back pocket and he was ready to use it. I felt sorry for him.

"We've only got a couple of minutes," I told him quietly. "You can do this."

In just a few seconds, he was dressed and ready. Well, he *looked* ready, but clothes couldn't fix everything.

"Just take a deep breath," I told him. "All you have to do is get through it, and I'm right here with you."

He closed his eyes. "Thanks, Owen," he said when he opened them again. "For everything."

"Ready?" I asked, and when he nodded, I led him out to

the gym, where Coach Baxter was standing at center court with his assistant, Mr. Webster.

"Welcome to tryouts," Coach said, looking from one guy to the next. "We're going to start with a few laps around the gym, then we'll get into drills. What I'm looking for today is some speed, stamina, and decent shooting."

Whew. I could handle that.

But could Russ? He didn't really have *any* of that stuff.

"Let's go!" Coach blew his whistle and we started to circle the gym.

By the end of the third lap, all of us had passed my brother. Twice.

Part of me wanted to slow down and jog with Russ. He was my twin, after all. But the other part knew that everyone in the gym was competing for a place on the team.

I was competing.

And I wasn't going to throw away my chance.

When I jogged past him again, I whispered, "Good job, Russ."

"I'm not fast enough," he gasped. His cheeks were red and he was already sweating.

"Just keep it slow and steady," I told him. "This isn't a race."

I thought about the stopwatch hanging from Coach's neck. The racing was later, but Russ didn't need to freak out about that yet.

By the end of the warm-up, we were all out of breath and sweaty, but only Russ looked like he was dying.

Or wished he was.

Forty-five minutes later, after a bunch of drills, most of us had finished running lines, and I'd just caught my breath when Coach asked, "Who's left?"

"Evans," Mr. Webster said. "Russell Evans."

"And?" Coach asked.

"That's it," Mr. Webster said, checking his clipboard.

"Okay, then. Evans, you're up."

Russell tucked his shirt into his shorts and moved away from the wall. He swallowed hard and walked to the line.

I gave him a thumbs-up as he went by, and I watched him get into starting position, his awesome Nikes toeing the line. He was all alone. With a crowd staring at him, waiting for him to fail. I took a deep breath, wishing I didn't have to watch.

And then it hit me. I *didn't* have to.

When I stood up and walked toward my brother, everyone started whispering, but I ignored them.

Russ jumped when I stepped onto the line next to him.

"What are you doing?" he asked.

I cleared my throat and told Coach, "I'll run with him."

"You're sure, Owen?" Coach asked.

"Yeah," I said, nodding.

"Okay, then." Coach blew the whistle.

As soon as we took off, I knew I'd done the right thing.

Russell was *super slow*, and if he'd run with anyone else, he would have been left in the dust in two seconds. I tried to forget that Coach was timing us and kept pace with Russ, so he wouldn't look bad.

But of course he looked bad.

He fell over twice when he bent to touch the lines, *and* he tripped over his shoelaces on the way back. He even stopped to retie them about halfway through, like Coach's stopwatch didn't even exist.

"Double knots," I hissed, then heard some of the guys laughing.

I had to keep reminding myself that Coach had already recorded my time, so I wasn't risking anything by helping my brother.

When we were finally finished, the stopwatch clicked, and Russell slid down the wall until he was sitting on the floor, with his head on his knees.

Coach Baxter growled, "Nice teamwork, Owen."

That felt good.

"Man," Chris said, shaking his head when I walked back to the guys. "It's like Russ was in slow motion."

"Yeah," Paul said, "like a replay on ESPN."

"And he doesn't mean a highlight," Nicky Chu added.

I glared at them and they dropped it.

Dribbling was next. Coach told us he wanted to check

out our ball-handling skills, but he was looking for control, not speed.

Lucky for Russ.

Coach split us into two groups, and we stood in front of the rows of orange cones Mr. Webster had put out.

"I want you to dribble through the cones and go in for a layup at the end," Coach explained. "Got it?"

I was near the end of the line, which was fine with me. When each of the guys ahead of me ran the drill, I watched closely to see what mistakes they made so I wouldn't make them, too.

Russell's turn was right before mine, and I heard more snickering.

Come on, Russ. Do it for us.

Coach blew the whistle and my twin took off. He managed to keep control of the ball, but barely. He knocked over three of his cones, but made it to the end.

When he went in for the layup, he totally missed the hoop.

"Air ball," Nicky Chu sang quietly, and a couple of guys laughed.

I didn't have time to worry about it, though, because I was up next.

When the whistle blew, I dribbled through the cones and made a perfect shot, off the backboard and through the net.

Yes!

We ran the same drill four more times, and I shot 100 percent. Seriously awesome!

Russell only made one basket, but he *did* leave all the cones standing on his last run. His tryout had started out stinking like old cheese, but it was getting better. Kind of.

"Okay," Coach said. "We know basketball is about scoring points, but it's also about defense."

I was relieved when he put me and Russ together for one-on-one.

"You ready?" I asked my brother.

"I missed every basket on that last drill," he said, and sighed.

"So what? *This* is what you do best. Remember what I told you the other day, about just standing there?"

Russ nodded.

"That's all you have to do. Just stand there and block my shots."

"But then you won't score, Owen."

Whoa! I hadn't thought of that. "Okay, let me make a couple of them."

For the next few minutes, I made Russell look like he had some idea what he was doing, which was good enough. With my help, he blocked about 75 percent of my shots.

Then it was my turn to defend the net against Russell. He slowly dribbled toward me, biting his lip. He checked the net, then looked back at me and came closer.

Just stay calm, Russ.

I bent my knees, ready.

He dribbled for a couple more seconds, and just when I thought he was going to go right, he lifted the ball in front of him and jumped straight up in the air.

He let the ball fly.

Stunned, I turned to watch it drop right into the net.

What?

The guys on the sidelines went nuts.

"Beautiful," Coach said, grinning. "Great form, kid. Give it another try."

Russell and I lined up face-to-face again.

"I can't believe I made that," he whispered to me, smiling.

"Me neither," I told him. What were the chances?

"I mean, that was a jump shot!"

"Yeah," I muttered, ticked off. How did he know that's what it was called? And weren't we supposed to be showing off *my* defense, not *his* shooting? "You made a jump shot."

And then, right in my face, he made seven more.

By the time my defensive "showcase" was over, I hadn't touched the ball once, and the rest of the guys were staring at Russ like he was a superhero.

No one said anything until Coach let out a quiet, "Wow."

Russ smiled, but he didn't look like he understood what had just happened.

I didn't either.

"Who taught you to shoot like that?" Mr. Webster asked.

I waited for Russ to say my name or point to me. I probably didn't wow anybody during the drill, but I could get some brownie points for teaching him everything he knew.

"No one," Russ said, shrugging.

What?

Of course, he was right. I couldn't do a jump shot myself, so there's no way I could have taught the most uncoordinated kid on the planet how to do one.

Or eight.

But still.

"You've just been practicing by yourself?" Coach asked.

"No," Russ said. He cleared his throat and I could tell he was embarrassed that everyone was staring at him. "That was my first try."

Coach's whistle fell out of his mouth. "Really?"

Russ shrugged.

Coach kept staring at my brother, like he couldn't believe it, then he shook his head. "Okay, everybody line up at center court."

We groaned, since we were way too tired for more drills.

But drills weren't what Coach had in mind.

"If you hear your name, you're on the team," he said, then waited for us to calm down before he announced, "Nicky Chu."

My old teammate waved his fist in the air and grinned.

Coach kept listing names and guys high-fived each other

when they were called. Most of the players had been on the team last year.

But not all of them.

I was just starting to get worried when Coach said, "Owen Evans."

"Yes!" I bumped fists with Chris, who'd already made it. We both jumped about four feet off the ground.

"Russell Evans," Coach said.

What?

If I could have frozen in midair, I would have. Instead, my second-class shoes hit the floor with a thud. I turned to stare at my brother, who looked as shocked as I was.

Russ made the team?

How was that even possible?

All I'd wanted to do was stop him from embarrassing me . . . I mean, *himself.*

When I thought about how much Russ stunk before he made those amazing shots, I felt like he'd tricked us.

Like he'd tricked me.

Russ turned toward me, and his smile was so big, I thought it might eat his whole face.

I kind of wished it would.

I took a deep breath and gave him a thumbs-up, trying to look like I really meant it.

But I didn't.

My brother and I walked home later that afternoon, side by side. My number five jersey was crammed into my bag. I'd wanted number eleven (Tim Camden's number), but like everything else lately, *Russ* got it.

"I can't believe it," he said, for the eight-millionth time. "I never thought I stood a chance."

"Me neither," I said, shoving my hands into my pockets.

"I owe it all to you," he said, quietly.

Yeah, he did. Why hadn't he just stood there, like I told him to? He wasn't supposed to *make* the stupid team!

"I think you're magical."

Huh? Magical?

I turned around to make sure no one had heard him. Then I looked at my twin, who was staring at his feet.

He wasn't even talking to me! He was thanking his stupid *shoes*!

"Are you kidding me?" I practically choked.

"What?"

I glared at him. "Never mind."

"Don't tell Dad I made it, okay?" he asked. "I want to do it."

I nodded. Yeah, Russ. You *just do it*.

You and your freakin' magical Nikes.

For the first time ever, I didn't want to talk about basketball when I got home.

"How did it go?" Dad asked, the second we walked through the door.

My brother made a big show of shaking his head and looking sad.

All I saw was more sneakiness.

"Russ?" Dad asked.

He shrugged. "I was the slowest guy at running lines."

"Oh no." Dad reached over to pat his shoulder. "I'm sorry."

My twin tried to hold back a laugh. "Sorry that I was slow, or sorry that I made the team, anyway?"

Suddenly he was a comedian, too? Jump shots? Punch lines? Mr. Hidden Talents rides again.

Dad stared at him. "What?"

"He made the team," Mom said, jumping up and down. Her eyes were shiny, like she might cry.

"*You* made the team," Dad said, slowly, still in shock. Then he grinned. "*You made the team!*"

He lifted his hand to give Russ a high five.

As usual, Russ missed.

"This is incredible," Dad said, pulling Russ into a hug. "We've got to celebrate. Let's go out for dinner."

"I was going to make spaghetti," Mom said, then smiled as she watched them. "Never mind. What about the Jade Palace?"

Great. Chinese food at my favorite restaurant, and I wasn't even hungry.

"Seriously?" Russ asked.

"Of course," Dad said, finally letting go of him. "You made the team, Russ. This is a night for celebration."

"I made the team, too," I said, but no one heard me. Was I invisible? In my own stinking house? "I made the team, too," I said, this time a lot louder. I sounded kind of mad actually, which made sense.

I *was* mad.

Everyone stopped to look at me, surprised.

"Of course you did," Dad said, slapping me on the back. "We knew you would. But this guy . . ." He turned back to Russ and wrapped an arm around his shoulder. "This guy just made my day."

Common Denominator

After so many years of being divided into brains and brawn, Owen and I had both been fine with our roles. But when Coach Baxter called my name, I realized that I'd only been fine with being the brains because I never imagined I could be *both* things—a mathlete and an . . . athlete.

Oh, I liked the sound of that!

I lifted the white tablecloth at Jade Palace, smiling at the sight of my Nikes.

They really were magical. And even more magical?

Dad was proud of me.

I didn't think I'd ever stop smiling, especially when I thought about those jump shots.

The truth was, I'd barely heard the guys cheering as

I made each one. When I'd thrown the ball, I hadn't been thinking about Owen, or making the Pioneers, or anything to do with basketball.

I'd been thinking about an egg.

Or, more specifically, a Masters of the Mind egg, thrown at just the right angle, with a built-in net for brakes.

I'd run through the list of challenge ingredients as I shot the ball again and again, trying to think of what we could use for our net.

$$\times \quad \div \quad +$$

Later that night, when we were back at the house, I got the call from Sara.

"How was the meeting?" I asked.

There was a short pause at the other end, before she said, "He's in."

"Arthur?" I asked, feeling an ounce or two of happiness leave my body. "He wants to join?"

"Yes," she sighed. "And he had a few ideas."

"For the fund-raiser?"

"Yes, but he also had a lot of ideas about how the meetings should be run and . . . that kind of thing."

"He's probably just trying to impress us," I told her. "We don't need to change anything. We have a great system already."

"I know," she said, but she didn't sound like she believed it.

"And the fund-raising?" I asked. "What's the plan?"

"We're having a bake sale."

"A what?" I choked.

"A bake sale."

"No, I heard you. I just . . . do any of us know how to bake?"

"I make pretty good peanut-butter cookies and Nitu's going to try an Indian dessert. Jason said his mom would probably help him with brownies."

"I'm sure my mom can help me make something, too." I waited for more, but she didn't say anything. "What about Arthur?"

"I'm not sure. We're hoping that whatever he brings doesn't have a Harvard emblem on it." She sighed. "You know, it wasn't easy, Russell. The meeting, I mean."

"It will get easier." We'd all adjust to Arthur because that was our only choice. It was as simple as that.

"The bake sale is this Friday afternoon," she said.

"Mr. Wills said it was okay?"

"Yes." She was quiet for a couple of seconds. "So, how did the tryouts go?"

"I made the team!" I couldn't help smiling as I said the words.

"Oh no," Sara said, then quickly added, "I mean, that's great, Russell. Good for you."

And it was.

Very good.

In the beginning, anyway.

✖   ➗   ➕

Even though the Masters team had already met that week, we decided to have another meeting on Thursday because there was so much to discuss. This time, I hosted and we met right after school so Nitu wouldn't be late for her father's birthday party.

After I received some stiff congratulations for making the basketball team, we got down to business.

But not before Arthur suggested, "We should have future meetings on Tuesdays and Fridays."

"Why?" Nitu asked, looking annoyed.

"Because the Friday meetings could run longer than the usual two hours. It's not a school night."

"But basketball games are on Fridays, aren't they, Russell?" Sara asked.

I nodded. "And practices are scheduled for Tuesdays and Thursdays, starting next week," I added. I knew that's why Arthur had suggested the change.

"That's going to take up a lot of time," Jason said.

"There's a time commitment, for sure," I told the group, "but you all know that Masters of the Mind is my priority."

"Except for yesterday," Arthur said smugly.

"That wasn't a regular meeting day," Nitu told him.

"I would have thought an emergency meeting was the most important kind," Arthur said.

"But you managed without me," I said, realizing too late that it was the wrong thing to say.

"Yes." Arthur smiled. "We managed perfectly well." He cleared his throat for dramatic effect. "Without you."

"Okay," I said, trying to move on. "So, it's decided. We'll keep our schedule the same." I looked at Nitu, who nodded. "Now, we've got the bake sale tomorrow, so we'll all have our treats ready and—"

"Speaking of treats," Mom said, appearing with a tray, "I've got milk and peanut-butter bars."

Sara, Nitu, Jason, and I all reached for glasses of milk and slices of Mom's specialty, while Arthur stayed in his seat.

Mom carried the tray over to him, but he shook his head. "I'm allergic to peanuts."

"Oh," Mom said. "I'm sorry. I'll find you something else."

"No, thank you." He sneered.

And that set the tone for the rest of the meeting. There was no smiling, no rhyming, and no kidding around.

By the time I told the team about the brilliant idea I had while I was making those jump shots, no one was in the mood to talk about the egg challenge. In fact, they seemed to stop listening as soon as I said the word basketball.

Later that evening I tracked Mom down in the den, where she was flipping through a magazine.

"Would you mind helping me with a baking fund-raiser?" I asked.

"Sounds fun." She smiled. "When is it?"

"Tomorrow."

She stared at me, then at her watch. "Are you kidding, Russell? It's past nine o'clock."

"I know. I'm sorry. I was distracted after my meeting and I forgot about it."

I didn't tell her that the distraction was trying on my Pioneers uniform and practicing jump shots in front of my bedroom mirror. I looked pretty good!

"Okay," she said, and sighed, getting up from her chair. "It would have been nice to know about this before your team ate all my peanut-butter bars, though, don't you think?"

"Good point." I winced.

"But let's see what we can whip up."

I followed her into the kitchen, where she checked the pantry for ingredients.

"What about chocolate-chip cookies?" she asked.

"Perfect." I would have happily agreed to anything she suggested.

She carried flour, salt, vanilla, and brown and white sugars over to the island in the middle of the kitchen.

"Can you please grab the butter and eggs, Russell?"

Uh-oh.

I opened the fridge door, hoping something had changed since I'd borrowed the challenge ingredients for my Masters meeting.

It hadn't.

"It looks like we're out of eggs," I told her.

"What? I had most of a carton in there."

"I had to use some for a Masters of the Mind project."

Mom rested one hand on her hip. "And what was this project?"

I explained the challenge, with plenty of detail, but Mom only focused on one fact.

"You threw half a dozen eggs out of Jason's window?"

"When you put it that way, it sounds wasteful," I told her.

"It *is* wasteful," Owen said as he moved past me to get the milk.

"Masters of the Mind is about science and experimentation," I explained, feeling defensive. "If there were no experiments, we'd never find cures for diseases or—"

"Hold on," Owen said, leaving the empty milk jug on the counter. "Are you saying that throwing eggs out of a window is going to cure cancer?"

"No," I snapped. "All I'm saying is—"

"All *I'm* saying," Mom interrupted, "is that no eggs means no cookies."

"What?"

"Russell, I can't bake anything without eggs. You should have given me more warning. Never mind the fact that you should have asked for permission before using the last of them."

"But I need the cookies for tomorrow." I couldn't let the team down! I was the leader! I had to do something. "Hold on."

I ran into the den and logged on to the Internet. My fingers flew over the keyboard as I searched. The first substitute I found for eggs in baking was milk. I shook my head and sighed with irritation. Owen had just guzzled the last of it.

And why was he being so cranky, anyway?

I didn't have time to worry about it.

I kept typing and within minutes, I was running back into the kitchen with great news.

"Applesauce!" I said.

"What?" Mom looked at me like I was speaking another language.

"Two-thirds of a cup of applesauce is equal to one egg."

She sighed. I was pretty sure she wanted to get back to her magazine.

"Please, help me," I begged.

And she did.

But that didn't mean the bake sale went according to plan.

✖   ➗   ➕

I carried my box of cookies to school on Friday, peeking at them every now and then to see if they looked any better.

They didn't.

When they'd come out of the oven looking gooey, Mom did an Internet search of her own.

It turned out that *one*-third of a cup of applesauce was equal to an egg.

Not *two*-thirds.

I was embarrassed that I hadn't double-checked.

Since we'd used all the applesauce and Mom said "no way" to a late-night trip to the grocery store, I was stuck with what Owen called "booger blobs" instead of cookies.

✖ ➗ ➕

Just before three o'clock, I looked over our table of "treats." Along with my soggy cookies and Jason's scorched brownies, we had small bowls of something definitely not solid and not quite liquid, prepared by Nitu and . . . that was it.

I leaned in for a closer look at the bowls.

"It's creamy phirni," our math whiz explained. "It's like chocolate pudding."

Except for the lumps.

"We're doomed," Jason whispered.

"What's in it?" I asked, ignoring him and hoping Nitu hadn't heard what he said.

"Rice," she said. "Try one."

I took one of her paper bowls and three plastic spoons, so Sara, Jason, and I could share.

It was incredible. Not too sweet, and super creamy.

"Wow!" I exclaimed.

"My grandmother's recipe," she said, smiling. "She makes it for special occasions."

"That's awesome!" Jason said, licking his spoon clean.

"Did you make the peanut-butter cookies?" I asked Sara, hopefully.

"Yes, but . . ." She had tears in her eyes.

"What's wrong?" I asked.

"I made them, but there was a complaint, so I can't sell them." Her face was bright red.

"A complaint from who?" I asked.

"*Whom*," Arthur Richardson the Third corrected, from behind me. "And the answer is me."

"What?" I choked.

"As I mentioned at the last meeting, I have a severe peanut allergy." He sniffed. "Even the dust can give me hives. Those cookies were like a plate of grenades."

I had to admit I liked the sound of that.

"He told Mr. Wills that his health was at risk," Nitu explained, shaking her head.

"I'm so sorry I won't be contributing to the bake sale," Sara said as a single tear rolled down her cheek.

I felt a headache coming on.

The heaviest element is copernicium.

The lightest is hydrogen.

I patted her arm. "You couldn't help it," I told her. I glanced at Arthur, who was looking a little too pleased with himself. "So, you got rid of the cookies but didn't bring anything of your own."

"Of course I did," Arthur said, with a smirk. "I'm waiting for my father's personal assistant to bring it in."

At that moment, a man in a pin-striped suit wheeled a cart down the hallway. It was loaded with boxes of Daley's Donuts.

"Oh man. I love those things," Jason said, licking his lips.

"My father owns six stores," Arthur said. "They're still warm."

"The stores?" Jason asked.

"The donuts," Arthur said, rolling his eyes.

"We can't sell those," Nitu said, shaking her head. "They're manufactured."

"Don't be ridiculous," Arthur told her. "They're fresh, delicious, *and* addictive."

"Selling bakery donuts goes against the whole concept of a bake sale," I told him.

Unfortunately, that was the moment the bell rang and school was out. The smell of fresh-baked donuts was irresistible, and within seconds, we were swamped with customers.

As the bake sale went on, the entire student body chose the donuts. I saw Nitu's expression change from hurt to angry and back to hurt again.

Sara handled sales and hurried the line along.

Jason and I took the payments, making change as quickly as we could while Nitu bagged treats.

And Arthur Richardson the Third?

For the next hour, he sat back and watched it all, like he was a supervisor and we were his employees.

When the final donut was gone and the last student left the building, we started cleaning up. Instead of helping, Arthur put himself in charge of counting the money.

"You were a huge help," Nitu told him, sarcastically.

"I made all the money." He shrugged.

"This was a *group effort*, Arthur," I reminded him.

He stared at the table, where all the homemade desserts still sat, untouched. "I beg to differ."

OWEN

Fast Break

During practices, Coach Baxter worked us even harder than he had at tryouts. The guy was tough!

I ran harder and faster than almost everyone and tried not to smile when my brother wound up at the back of the pack in nearly everything we did. It served him right.

About halfway through one practice, Coach blew his whistle and we got in a line for layups.

I made my first shot, then passed the ball to Paul, who missed his. I jogged back to the end of the line to wait for another turn.

Then Coach Baxter left Mr. Webster in charge, and he took Russell over to the far basket. While I waited for my turn to shoot, I watched Coach. I hoped he realized he'd made a huge mistake and was cutting Russ from the team in private.

But I was disappointed.

The two of them spent the next hour working on Russ's dribbling skills.

Well, lack of dribbling skills, really.

Man, I would have loved to get some one-on-one time with Coach! But it was all about Russ.

Everything was about Russ.

I kept checking over my shoulder to watch them, and it was obvious that my brother wasn't getting it.

Coach looked like he was losing patience, or maybe I just hoped he was.

"Owen," Chris shouted, right as a basketball hit the side of my head.

"Sorry, man," Paul said, jogging toward me. "I thought you knew I was passing it to you."

"That was a *pass*?" I growled.

"I *said* I was sorry," Paul said. "Hey, you're supposed to be keeping your eye on the ball, anyway."

"Whatever," I muttered, rubbing my head.

"Whatever, yourself." Paul shook his head as he walked to the back of the line.

When I took my next turn, I moved in for the perfect layup, but the ball bounced off the bottom of the rim then hit me.

In the face.

"Nice one," someone whispered.

"Which Evans twin is that?" someone else asked, a little louder, and I heard some of the other guys laughing.

I passed the ball to Nate and walked to the back of the line. I didn't make eye contact with the rest of my teammates and tried not to watch Russ and Coach Baxter either. I folded my arms and waited for my next turn.

Basketball was supposed to be *fun*.

I had to get my brother out of my head.

Fast.

It felt like everything was changing in the worst way. Even though I knew it wouldn't be a big deal to anyone else, I hated that Russ suddenly had the cool shoes *and* the awesome jump shot.

We were supposed to be opposites.

The jock and the brains.

We couldn't *both* be jocks and we couldn't trade places.

I mean, what was the chance of me turning into a genius overnight?

Zip.

At the end of practice, Coach brought Russell back over to the rest of us.

"Our first game is on Friday. That doesn't give us much time before we face Westhill's team."

"They're tough," Chris said, like we didn't all know that already.

"What we're going to do at each practice is run drills for the first half and scrimmage for the second. Everybody got that?" Coach asked.

I nodded along with the rest of the guys.

"One weakness we've got is stamina," Coach continued.

At least four guys turned to look at Russ, who practically ran out of breath walking to the bathroom.

"I'm talking about the team as a *whole*," Coach said, giving us all the stare down. "Stamina is key, here. We have to be able to keep up."

The guys nodded again.

"Now, let's get that scrimmage going."

The next night, I had an English paper to work on, and I didn't feel like it at all. We were supposed to write five hundred words on someone who inspired us.

Obviously, I was going to write about Tim Camden. He was an awesome player, scored tons of points, and did what needed to be done to win the game.

But I was having trouble getting the ideas out of my brain and into my notebook.

I decided to head for the park to shoot some hoops and clear all the junk out of my head. When I called Chris to go with me, there was no answer at his house. So I decided to go on my own, hoping some of the guys would be there.

I dribbled the ball all the way to the park, trying to think about the "inspiration" paper, but all I could think about was Russ and how mad I was at him.

When I got to Sunset, a bunch of teenagers were already playing on the main court.

Great.

I bent over to retie my laces before heading back home.

"Hey, you wanna play?" someone shouted.

I went for my usual double knots.

"You wanna play?" the voice shouted again, even louder.

I looked up to see who they were talking to, and gulped when I saw that the teenagers were all staring at me.

"Me?" I asked, my voice shaking a bit.

They never talked to us. They never even looked at us.

"You're the only one out there," a big guy said, laughing. "We're short a man."

"Short a man?" I repeated.

Could they really be asking me to fill in?

High school kids?

"Yeah," the guys said.

"And you want me to—"

"Forget it," a skinny redhead interrupted. "There's something wrong with him."

"No, there isn't," I said, standing up.

I didn't know what to do.

The idea of playing with the teenagers was totally scary.

But it was also totally cool.

What if some of the Pioneers showed up and saw me hanging out with them?

That would be *awesome*.

"So?" the big guy asked.

Yes, please probably wouldn't sound very cool.

"Sure," I said, trying to act like it was no big deal as I jogged toward the court.

"This should be good," the redhead groaned.

"I'm Matt," the big guy said. "You, me, Rick, Devinder, and Jonesy are a team."

When he said each name, the guys nodded at me, so I'd know who they were. I waited for them to ask for my name, but nobody seemed to care.

They just called me "kid."

For the next hour, I worked even harder than I had at practice. I was at least a foot shorter than everyone else, and I really had to sweat to keep up.

The guys didn't pass to me much at first, and I started to wonder why they'd even invited me to play. What was the point of being an extra body if you didn't get to *do* anything?

Then Jonesy threw me the ball and I knew it might be my only chance to prove myself.

Two big guys came at me, and I took a deep breath, slowly dribbling in place until I saw the opening I was looking for. I made a break for it, shouldering the guy on the right and squeezing between them.

"What the . . . ?" one of them grunted from behind me.

I was out in the open, only a few steps from the basket.

I knew my safest bet was a layup, so I dribbled in fast and made it.

"Nice!" Matt said, slapping me on the back. "You're a tough kid. I like it."

I grinned.

I liked it, too.

From then on, whenever the guys gave me the ball, I pushed through whoever was in my way. I used my shoulders and elbows and went straight to the hoop.

Just like Tim Camden.

It was rougher than the Pioneers played, but it worked.

"A go-to guy," Rick said, after I made another shot. "Give the kid the ball, and he makes it happen."

"You've got to be aggressive to win, right?" Matt said, punching me on the shoulder.

"Yeah." I nodded.

Aggressive.

I'd never thought about basketball that way before.

The Pioneers didn't have a "go-to guy." We just passed the ball around until somebody had a clear shot. We were all about teamwork, not star players, and I knew that was a good thing.

But I also knew that going for the basket had way better results.

After all, basketball was about scoring points, and no one got points for *passing*.

Back at school the next day, I met up with Chris at his locker so we could walk to English class together.

"I'm almost finished writing my inspiration paper," he said. "It's about my uncle Eddy. You know, the one who was in that car accident?"

"And they said would never walk again?"

Chris nodded. "Yeah. Now he's running."

"Pretty cool."

"What about you?" he asked.

"I haven't started," I admitted. "But I'm going to write about Tim Camden."

Chris laughed. "The most hated guy in the NBA."

"But an awesome player."

"Totally," he agreed. "Hey, I got your message last night. I wish I'd made it to the park, but we had to go visit my cousins."

"Too bad," I told him.

And I meant it. I'd met his cousins.

"Did you find anyone to play with?"

I nodded and told him about the teenagers.

"You and the big kids?" he asked, squinting at me like he wasn't sure whether to believe it.

"High school guys," I corrected, loving the sound of it. Me and the high school guys, kickin' it. "Yeah."

"They just . . . asked you to play?"

"Well, they were short a guy, so . . . ," I said, and shrugged.

Chris stared at me. "That is *so* cool."

"It was okay," I told him.

Of course, it was way better than okay. It was ESPN highlight material.

When Chris told some of the other Pioneers about it, I told them how I'd driven to the net a bunch of times. (Well, three times, anyway, scoring twice). And how when the teenagers left, Matt and Jonesy both high-fived me on their way off the court.

Unreal!

The way the guys were looking at me, I could tell they'd forgotten about Russ, and that was awesome.

"Are you going to play with them again?" Chris asked.

The teenagers hadn't said anything about it, but I didn't care.

"Maybe a pickup game here and there," I told him, shrugging again.

It wasn't impossible, right?

"Whoa," he whispered.

The rest of the week raced by, and even though I was mad that Russ was there, the practices weren't bad.

The drills were brutal, but I "borrowed" Russ's digital watch so I could measure my improvements. And I was definitely improving. I was getting faster at running lines, and even though it was the drill I hated the most, I was proud of being one of the fastest guys on the team. The scrimmages were my favorite part of practices, and it was pretty cool to see our passing game coming together, too.

I kept an eye on Russ, who was getting a little better at dribbling.

Better than a seven-year-old, anyway.

Maybe.

Even though Russ and I left basketball on the court, Dad liked to relive our practices at the dinner table every night. And while Russell did all the talking, Dad acted like he was the most interesting person on earth.

I just concentrated on my vegetables.

Mom must have noticed something was up, because on Thursday, the night before our first game, she made me stay with her in the kitchen to help put away the dishes.

"Everything okay with you, Owen?" she asked.

"Yup."

"How's the team?"

"Basketball?" I asked.

"Yes," she laughed. *"Basketball."*

"It's fine."

Mom put a hand on my forehead.

"What?" I asked.

"I'm just checking for a fever. It's usually 'awesome.'"

"I know . . . it's just kind of . . . different this year."

"Ahh," she said. "A new coach."

I didn't want to talk about the whole mess with Russell, so I just nodded.

"Don't worry, honey. You'll get used to him." She handed me some glasses to put away. "Dad and I are excited about tomorrow's game."

"Me, too," I told her.

I was excited, but kind of nervous, too.

I had no idea what would happen.

Complex Division

My week was a blur of basketball practices, Masters meetings, and my usual workload from school. I'd like to say I floated through it all with the greatest of ease, but the truth was, my hectic schedule was causing some problems.

I got a ninety on my science test.

Barely an A!

I didn't have time to proofread my English essay before I handed it in, and I should have *made* the time. Mrs. Chen found two spelling mistakes, and there was a concerned note on the top of my cover page when she handed it back to me with a big red B on it.

And worst of all? I missed another Masters of the Mind meeting because Coach wanted to squeeze in an extra practice before our first game.

When the day of the Pioneers' first game arrived, I woke up feeling more than a little nervous. I'd been surviving the practices and even surprised myself with some great moments, but playing against another team was something totally new.

And playing that game in a gymnasium packed with fans, demanding a win? That was very intimidating.

But throughout the day, I was high-fived by every member of the basketball team I saw. It was a complete surprise and I couldn't help grinning whenever it happened.

I felt like I was really part of something.

Of course, I'd already felt like part of my other clubs and Masters of the Mind, but this was different. People who never paid attention to me before suddenly noticed me.

I liked it.

When I suited up with the rest of the team in the locker room after school, I could feel the tension in the air. Obviously I wasn't the only one battling nerves.

"Are you ready, Russ?" Nicky Chu asked me.

"I hope so," I told him.

"You'll be fine," he said, slapping me on the back.

It was more than Owen had said to me all week. I didn't know why my brother was so quiet, but I assumed he'd been busy, like me.

Coach gave us a pep talk before the game started, then I spent the first quarter watching my teammates play from the bench.

The view was amazing.

But the playing wasn't.

The Westhill team had a better record than the Pioneers, and they were living up to their reputation as a tough team to beat. We were losing, but I could see how hard my team-mates were trying and I was proud of them.

Every now and then, I'd wave at my parents in the stands, knowing how happy they were to see me out there.

The rest of the time, I couldn't help admiring my magical Nikes.

By the end of the quarter, I guessed Coach would keep me on the bench while his more experienced players tried to catch up to Westhill. And that was fine with me. I didn't need that kind of pressure during my very first game.

But I was wrong.

"I'm gonna mix things up," Coach said.

And that meant putting me in.

For the first few minutes I was out on the court, I was lost. Everything seemed louder, brighter, and faster than it had at practice. I tried to "just stand there," but the Westhill team was pretty good at dribbling around me.

At one point, Paul was heading for the basket and I chased after him, hoping I could somehow stop one of the Westhill players from blocking his shot.

When I stopped, there was no one anywhere near me. There was nothing but open space between me and the hoop.

"Paul," I shouted, before I could change my mind. "Over here!"

He turned and threw me the ball.

I knew I only had a couple of seconds before the Westhill players would surround me, so I did the only thing I could think of.

I took a jump shot.

And scored three whole points!

The only words I heard over the roar of the crowd was Coach shouting, "Nice hustle, Russell!"

I couldn't believe how different everything was after that first game.

Dad couldn't stop smiling.

Mom gave me a huge hug and told me how proud she was.

Owen didn't say anything.

Not "way to go" or "nice job" or even "you didn't blow it."

He was *silent*.

When his friend Chris came over on Saturday morning, I answered the door as I was getting ready for my Masters of the Mind meeting.

"Russ!" Chris said, punching my shoulder like I'd seen the jocks do to each other. It kind of hurt. "How's it going?"

"Good," I said, surprised that he hadn't just grunted hello and headed for Owen's room the way he usually did.

"Cool," he said. "I still can't believe how awesome you played yesterday. Westhill didn't know what hit them."

"Thanks," I said, grinning. I knew I needed to get going but thought that talking about basketball for a minute or two might be fun.

"I mean, for your first real game, that was pretty sweet."

"Are you coming up?" Owen asked from the top of the stairs.

"Just a sec," Chris called back, then turned to me again. "Can you teach me some of your moves?"

"My moves?"

"Yeah, that jump shot is awesome."

"You want *me* to teach *you*?" I asked, stunned.

"Sure. You help me with the jump shot and I'll help you with your dribbling."

"Chris!" Owen called again.

"I'm coming," Chris answered. "Maybe we should stay late after practice sometime and—"

"Chris!" Owen shouted.

"Geez, I'm coming!" He punched my shoulder again. "We'll figure something out later, Russ."

I smiled as I finished gathering my Masters materials together and said good-bye to Mom.

Sara's house was close enough that I could walk, and all

the way there, I thought about the unexpected things basketball was doing for me. It was building my confidence. I was making new friends. And most amazing of all? I was having fun.

"Hey, Russell," Sara said when she opened her front door.

"Sorry I'm late," I told her. "I was talking to one of the basketball guys. You know, about the game last night."

"I heard about it," she said.

"Thanks," I told her, then realized she hadn't complimented my playing. Embarrassed, I quickly said, "I mean, it was a good game."

"I'm glad," she said, but she didn't sound very enthusiastic. "Everyone is downstairs."

I would have liked to tell her about my big play, but I quietly followed her instead.

"There he is," Nitu said when we walked into the TV room. The rest of the team was already there, waiting. "The basketball star."

"In person," I said, grinning.

"And late," Arthur Richardson the Third said, pointing to his watch. "I thought we agreed to meet at ten, Russell."

"We did."

"Then why are you arriving at seven minutes past?"

"Sorry, I was just—"

"We don't need an excuse," Arthur said, rolling his eyes. "We need everyone to be on time."

"Sure, but . . ." I glanced at Nitu, who shook her head like it was pointless to argue with him. It probably was.

Jason cleared his throat, looking uncomfortable. "How about we start with some word problems?"

"I was thinking we should take another run at the egg drop," I told him. "I think the idea I came up with could work and—"

"Could? We need an idea that *will* work," Arthur interrupted. "And speaking of ideas, there's something I'd like to discuss with the group."

"What now?" Nitu asked, rolling her eyes.

"Leadership."

"What about it?" I asked, my whole body tense.

Tungsten, vanadium, manganese.

He stared at me. "I think this team needs some."

"We have a leader," Sara said, softly, glancing at me.

"I mean full-time."

"What are you—" I began, but he interrupted me.

"In the short period of time I've been part of this team, you've missed two meetings, left your brain at home during the Beaumont practice session, and seem to be much more interested in basketball than anything else."

"That's not true," I told him.

"I think this team needs to consider electing a new leader."

"Who, you?" I snapped.

"Is that a nomination?" he asked.

"No." I looked at Nitu, then at Jason and Sara. "Is this how all of you feel?" I asked, through the lump in my throat.

"No," Nitu said. "You're a great team leader." She glared at Arthur.

"Jason?" I asked.

"Uh," he said, looking even more uncomfortable than before. "You have seemed kind of, uh, distracted, and the district competition is coming up fast."

I stared at him, but he wouldn't meet my eyes. "What about you, Sara?" I asked the quietest member of the team.

She bit her lip for a second or two before answering. "Your basketball schedule seems pretty busy, you know?" She bit her lip again.

Arthur smirked.

"It's going to be fine," Nitu told the group. "Russell can handle it, can't you?"

I nodded, but knowing that part of the team had lost confidence in me, I wasn't so sure.

"We can talk about it later," Arthur said. "Just like the egg challenge. In the meantime," he said, "let's get started on some word problems, right, Jason?"

It was like he'd already taken over.

Intentional Foul

In between our first and second games, when I was feeling madder than ever at Russ, I started thinking about Tim Camden even more than usual. The guy made plays and points, period. Sure, he might not have been everyone's hero, but he was a go-to guy. And that was more important than being liked.

So, I'd decided that the best way to handle the Russell situation was to be just like Camden.

"Are you ready?" Russell asked, meeting up with me and Chris on the way to the gym on game day.

I didn't say anything.

"Sure," Chris told him. "This one's in the bag."

An eighth grader was standing outside the gym when we got there. "Let's see that hustle, Russell," she said, smiling up at him.

"Uh, sure." Russ's cheeks turned red.

"Man, everyone's into it," Chris said, chuckling. "All I've been hearing about is the Russell Hustle."

When we walked into the gym, I saw what he meant.

There were signs all over place. Sure, a bunch said "Pioneers Rule" and stuff like that, but tons of them were about Russell and his hustle.

"Mom and I got off work early for the game," Dad said, climbing up the bleachers and grinning. "The Russell Hustle. We love it!"

"Yeah, it's awesome," I said, gritting my teeth. "I'd better go get changed."

I was sick of everything. The three-pointers, the jump shots, the Nikes, and now the Russell Hustle.

I had to make my mark on the game. It was time to leave my brother in the dust.

But at tip-off, I was stuck on the bench.

Meanwhile, Mr. Hustle was at center court, in front of a chanting crowd. The way things were going, he'd probably be riding a float home after the game.

When the ref blew his whistle, I watched Russ jump and tap the ball toward Paul, who got double-teamed by two of the Eagles.

"Somebody open up for him," Coach Baxter shouted. "Help him out!"

Nate tried to lose the guy who was guarding him, but couldn't get away.

"Keep moving, guys!" Coach shouted.

Suddenly, Russ ran down the court and made a hard left, his awesome Nikes squeaking against the hardwood.

"I'm open!" he shouted.

You've got to be kidding me.

Paul spun around and threw him the ball.

Russ was smart enough to stay where he was, instead of messing everything up by trying to dribble.

I wanted to close my eyes, but I couldn't help watching him make that stupid jump shot.

Again.

Swish.

"Nice hustle, Russell!" some girls screamed from the middle of the bleachers.

Didn't anyone see that he had no skills? Sure, he could shoot, but he wasn't even *moving* with the ball.

One of the Eagles took a shot, and it bounced off the rim. Paul and Nicky battled the point guard for the ball, but the Eagles ended up with possession.

The scuffle gave Russ just enough time to jog down the court in slow motion. When the Eagle lined up his shot and let go of the ball, Russell blocked it.

Somebody in the stands shouted "Denied!" and that got the cheers going again.

Nate grabbed the loose ball and took off toward the Skyline Eagles' basket. He missed his shot and the crowd groaned until Russell caught the rebound. He threw the ball and I held my breath, watching it fly through the air.

And miss the hoop.

I let out the breath.

Whew!

Coach called a time-out and the guys came in for a huddle.

"Russ, you're a dynamo," Coach said, slapping him on the back. "Great teamwork out there, all of you. I really like what I'm seeing." He saw my brother panting. "Russell, hit the bench. Owen, take center."

Awesome.

It was my turn to rock the gym.

Half a second in, I snatched the ball from one of the Eagle guards and took off down the court. They thought Russell could hustle? They hadn't seen anything yet.

I was the go-to guy, just like the teenagers said.

"I'm open!" I heard Paul shout.

I bounced the ball off the backboard and into the net.

Yes! Two points for the *other* Evans brother, thank you very much. And I was just getting started.

I ran backward toward our net, keeping an eye on the ball as one of the Eagles dribbled toward center court, then crossed the line. He looked to his left and I knew he was going to pass. At the last second, I stole the ball.

The crowd cheered when I raced back down the court.

"Over here," Nate yelled.

I took the shot. Another two points for me!

I mean, the team.

Either way, I was on fire!

"Are you deaf?" Nate asked me, as we ran back down the court.

"What?"

"Very funny."

"Hey, they were easy shots, so I took them."

Geez. If *he* wanted to make the shots, *he* should have been the one stealing the ball.

I couldn't do everything.

Or could I?

Once we had possession again, Nate threw the ball more *at* me than *to* me. I took off with it, shouldering past one of the Eagle players, but another one stood between me and the basket.

"Pass it!" Coach Baxter shouted from the sidelines.

Forget that, I was in perfect position! I crouched and eyeballed the basket.

"I'm open," Paul shouted, over the sound of the crowd.

I ignored him and threw the ball. It flew through the air, heading straight for the net.

But didn't get there.

"Air ball!" the Eagles fans sang.

And that was when Coach called another time-out.

"Ball hog," Paul muttered as we walked over to the bench.

Coach's face was bright red. "Didn't you hear me, Owen? I told you to pass."

"Sorry," I told him. "I thought I could make it."

Nate and Paul both glared at me.

Russell patted me on the back and whispered, "It was a good try, Owen."

I didn't need to hear it from him! Good try? I'd already put us in the freakin' lead.

"Let's share the ball out there, okay?" Coach was looking straight at me.

The buzzer sounded and we were back in the game.

I thought about sharing, but why miss out on easy baskets?

The next time I got the ball, I drove to the net. Two more points.

"You're not Camden," Paul said.

"I never said I was."

"Well, you're acting like him."

"Yeah," Nate agreed. "And remember the Blazers traded him."

"For *two guys*." I waved two fingers at them. "It took two guys to replace him."

"Yeah, but now the Blazers are winning," Paul said.

"So are we," I growled, pointing at the scoreboard.

After a few more minutes, Russell was back in. He waved at me, but I just nodded back. I could feel my stomach tensing up, being on the court with him.

When he made another stupid jump shot, the crowd cheered, louder than they'd cheered for me.

One of the Eagle guards stole the ball from Nate, but when he missed a shot, I picked up the rebound and took off.

"Russell's open!" Coach Baxter shouted from the sidelines.

"Pass it!" Chris yelled, keeping pace beside me.

That's when I tripped and lost the ball.

Russell caught it and started trying to dribble toward the basket.

Not another shot! It was *my* turn!

I ran over to him. "Give it."

"Huh?" He squinted at me through his smudged glasses.

The fans were so loud, I had to shout. "Give me the ball!"

"But—"

In mid-bounce, I grabbed it.

I swear the whole crowd gasped, but I didn't care. I turned toward the net.

"Let Russell shoot!" somebody shouted.

But I *couldn't* do that. Not again.

The ball bounced off the rim, and the crowd groaned.

Coach Baxter called a time-out and started yelling at me before I even got to the bench. "You're out of the game!"

"What?" I choked.

The crowd started booing, and I was sure they were mad at Coach for pulling me. Then I realized they were actually booing *me*. The guy who was working harder than anyone to win the game!

While I sat on the bench, Coach let me have it.

"What are you trying to do out there?" He was so mad his mouth was foaming, and there were bits of spit flying everywhere. "No passing?" he asked.

"We needed points, and I got, like, twelve."

"And lost us just as many," Coach barked.

None of the guys said anything. They just stood there.

"Have you ever heard that there's no 'I' in teamwork?" Coach asked.

I'd had enough. Didn't anyone see how much I was doing for the team? "Yeah, but there's an 'I' in points," I told him.

"What did you say?" he asked, leaning toward me.

"Uh-oh," Chris whispered.

Russell shook his head, like I should stop.

But I wasn't finished. "There's one in *points*, one in *win* . . ." I thought for a second. "And there's one in *victory*."

"Don't forget there's one in idiot," Paul muttered.

"Two, actually," Russell told him.

I shot him a dirty look. "Thanks."

"Well, there are," Russ said.

Coach took a deep breath. "What you boys just witnessed was the worst show of sportsmanship I have ever seen."

Great.

"Did Jordan ever hog the ball like that?" Nate asked.

"Jordan?" Coach asked, looking confused.

"Michael Jordan," Nate said. "Did he hog the ball when you coached him?"

"Hold on," Coach said. "Who said I coached Michael Jordan?"

"Owen," three guys said at once.

"What?" Coach stared at me.

I cleared my throat. "Okay, I didn't actually say you coached him. I just . . . didn't say you *didn't*."

Everyone was quiet.

"Well, I didn't coach Michael Jordan," Coach Baxter said. "And here's an interesting fact you might want to consider. In his sophomore year of high school, nobody did."

"What?" Chris asked.

"He got cut from the team," Coach Baxter said, then looked at me. "Which is exactly where you're headed if you don't shape up."

The buzzer went off and the guys headed back out to the court. Chris took my position, while I sat on the bench.

We ended up winning the game, thanks to Russell's *seventeen* points and eight rebounds.

I took off right at the final buzzer, wanting to get out of there as fast as I could. I'd almost finished stuffing my gear into my bag when the rest of the team caught up with me.

"Nice game, Owen," Paul said. "I never knew basketball was a solo sport."

I didn't say anything.

"Why didn't you just share the ball?" Chris asked.

I shrugged. "I wanted to win."

"Oh yeah?" Paul asked. "Well, so did we."

Russell was the last guy into the locker room, and he didn't look at me or say anything. He just sat on the bench and took off his shoes.

"You were the *hero*, man," Nate said, grinning and slapping him on the back. "Seventeen points. That's awesome!"

The guys crowded around Russell, and his face got all red.

When they all started high-fiving him, I knew I had to get out of there before I puked. I walked along the back of the bench, and that's when I saw them.

The Nikes.

I checked over my shoulder to make sure no one was looking and picked them up off the floor. I shoved them into my bag, and instead of climbing the stairs to meet Mom and Dad, I opened the custodian's door and went outside.

There was no one around, so I ran around the corner to the Dumpster behind the cafeteria and pulled the shoes out of my bag.

I didn't even have to think about what I did next.

I threw them into the Dumpster and heard a splat.

Gross.

I ran back to the locker room, like nothing had happened, and raced through to the gym before anybody noticed me.

"Not your best game," Dad said when I met him in the stands. "You've got to start passing."

"I was just trying to win," I told him. Why did I have to keep explaining that?

"You'll do better next time," Mom said, giving me a hug.

"Where's Russell?" Dad asked.

"Right here," he said from behind me.

I couldn't help checking his feet, hoping he'd brought another pair of shoes.

Whew.

Loafers.

When I looked up again, Russ was staring at me.

"You were phenomenal!" Dad said, pulling him into a hug.

"Seventeen points," Mom said. "Just fantastic!"

"We should go out for dinner, to celebrate," Dad said, rubbing his belly.

My stomach was growling and I thought a big juicy hamburger might help me forget my time on the bench, so—

"Would it be okay if we just went home?" Russell asked. "I'm not feeling very well."

"Is it your tummy?" Mom asked.

I checked to make sure no one heard her. We didn't say "tummy" in middle school.

We said gut, and mine was ready for some greasy french fries.

"Kind of," Russ said, staring at me.

That's when my juicy hamburger went out the window.

Russ and I sat in the backseat for the drive home, and while Mom and Dad talked about the great game, Russ stared straight ahead and I stared at my hands.

"You two made quite the team out there," Mom said.

"Well, they would have, if Owen had passed Russ the ball a few times," Dad said.

"Or once," Russ muttered.

"What's that, honey?" Mom asked.

"Nothing," he said, quietly.

"I'm sorry you aren't feeling well," she said, looking at him in the rearview mirror. "I've got chicken at home. I'll make you some soup."

"Thanks, Mom," he said.

Whatever.

He'd ended up being the hero of the game while I rode the stinkin' bench!

And did he even care?

The guy had only been playing basketball for a couple of weeks, and he had all his other junk, like Masters of the Mind and Math Club to keep him busy.

The only thing I had in the world was basketball.

And I was starting to lose it.

Boiling Point

On the way home, I had no interest in talking about the game, but that didn't stop my parents. While they talked, I tried to understand what Owen had done.

My brother and I didn't always see things the same way, and my idea of fair didn't always line up with his. I hated to say it, but sometimes Owen could be a bit . . . selfish. I tried to ignore it, because he had so many other great qualities, but when I thought about the way he'd taken those Nikes, it all came rushing back to me.

There were the bicycles my grandparents had given us for our birthdays in the second grade. I took special care of mine to make sure it always looked as good as new. But when Owen crashed his identical bike into a fence while he was goofing around, bending the fender and scratching the paint down one side, he secretly swapped it for mine in the garage. He put a sticker with his name on it under the seat and pretended it had been his all along.

The sad part was, I would have traded him if he'd just asked me.

I could think of a hundred different cases just like that one, where Owen took the best without thinking about anyone else's feelings.

He took Dad's big gym bag when Mom told me I could use it for school. He drank the last of the milk. He hogged the TV. He "borrowed" things (like my digital watch) and never gave them back. He wouldn't even share his friends by letting me talk to Chris the other morning.

And now the shoes.

I could still picture his face when he came back into the locker room after taking them. Why did he even bother hiding them in his gym bag? Was I supposed to frantically search for them, like I did when I was eight and he buried the best astronaut from my Lego space station in the backyard? Or was it more like the game of "keep away" older kids used to play with my rock-identification kit at recess? Was I supposed to beg and plead with him to give me my beloved shoes back?

After all the hard work I'd put in and winning points I'd earned for the Pioneers, I would have thought I'd earned some respect, too. I was supposed to be one of the guys now. I was supposed to have cool gear.

Why did Owen want to ruin that?

As much as loved my brother, I was angry and disappointed that he was trying to play tricks. Especially when he knew how important those shoes were to me.

We drove past Jade Palace and I thought about that celebration dinner just the other night. Owen had grabbed the last egg roll without asking anyone else if they wanted it. I'd been in such a good mood at the time, I barely noticed, but now that I'd seen how mean he could be, I remembered.

I wiggled my toes. They felt strange in my loafers, like they weren't at home anymore.

I wondered how long Owen would wait to give me the Nikes back. Would he drag it out for a day? Two? Would he tuck the bag under his bed and wait until minutes before game time to whip them out from his hiding place? Or would he wait even longer?

No, he knew those shoes were the secret to my success on the court.

Hmm. That got me wondering even more.

Did he steal them to *stop* me from playing basketball?

I didn't want to think so.

When I made the Pioneers roster, it felt like a dream I never knew existed had come true. I'd felt like I was part of something totally new and different and that I could be more than anyone expected. I was happy when I put on that jersey, when kids wished me luck in the hallway before the game and when the crowd cheered for me.

And Owen didn't like it.

In fact, I was beginning to think he hated it.

I closed my eyes.

There were so many things racing around in my mind, I couldn't focus on any of them. My stomach was in knots, thinking about all the different expectations people had of me.

Mom and Dad wanted me to be a basketball star.

Owen wanted me to fail.

Three Masters of the Mind members wanted me to give up basketball.

Arthur just wanted me to give up leadership.

But what did I want?

I thought about it for a second and the answer was obvious.

Most of all, I wanted those Nikes back.

When we got home, I knew Owen would go straight for his basketball. I also knew it was out in the garage, so I got there first.

When he came to get it, I was ready for him.

"Looking for this?" I asked.

"Yeah," he said, making a grab for the ball.

But I wasn't ready to hand it over. I wanted answers.

"Why wouldn't you pass to me today?" I demanded.

"What?"

"You heard me."

"I wanted to win." He rolled his eyes. "Why doesn't any-body get that?"

"But you didn't even make all your shots." I stared at him, wondering what he'd done with his gym bag. "In fact, I had a higher shooting percentage than you did."

"Yeah, well you had more time on the court."

"Only because you refused to be a team player and got taken out of the game," I said quietly. There was a warning in my voice, but somehow he didn't hear it.

I asked him why he'd actually *stolen* the ball from me.

Of course, I was pretty sure I knew the answer, but I wanted to hear him say it.

"Why don't you want me to play?" I demanded.

"Why'd *you* have to take all those shots? I told you from the very beginning that all you had to do was stand there!"

For the first time in my life, I could have punched him. "Maybe I didn't *want* to just stand there, Owen. Maybe I wanted to play the game like everybody else."

"But—"

"You're the only person who told me to stand there, you know. Coach didn't say that. Dad didn't say that." I paused. "Nobody else said that. Why do you want me to fail?

"I never said—"

"You don't have to say it, Owen. I can tell."

"You don't know what you're talking about. You and your stupid Russell Hustle."

I couldn't believe what I was hearing. "*That's* why you're mad? Because I have a rhyme?"

It was almost funny. Almost.

"Maybe you had a rhyme already, Russ. Like Geek of the Week."

I'd had enough. "Where are they?"

"Who?" he asked.

My fists were clenched by my sides. "My shoes, Owen."

He paused, then told me, "In the Dumpster behind the cafeteria."

I felt like I'd been punched.

The Dumpster?

Those beautiful shoes? The most expensive things I'd ever owned? He'd thrown them into a pile of stinking, rotting garbage?

I thought I might be sick.

I wanted to tackle him or swear at him or something even worse. But I couldn't do any of those things.

Instead, I threw the ball at him. Hard.

"*Oof,*" he grunted, catching it against his stomach.

"You know what, Owen? You're a total jerk," I told him, then walked away before I could do or say anything worse.

OWEN

Time-out

I don't know why, but Russ calling me a jerk felt worse than a swear word. It felt worse than a kick in the pants or a fist to the gut.

"Well, so are you," I yelled after him, but he was already back inside the house. "The Russell Hustle," I muttered. "It's not my fault nothing rhymes with Owen."

"I know something that does," Dad said, from behind me.

When I turned around and saw his face, I knew he'd heard everything.

"What?" I asked.

"Mowin'. And that's what you're going to be doing for the next eight Saturdays."

"Are you kidding me?" I choked. "We're supposed to share chores."

"You're supposed to share a lot of things," he said quietly. "Including the spotlight from time to time."

"But—"

"I figure eight Saturdays is about how long it'll take to earn enough money to replace those shoes."

"Come on, Dad, I—"

"Acted like the most selfish kid on the court, then destroyed your brother's property?"

"Well, he's destroying my life."

Dad snorted, like that was the dumbest thing he'd ever heard. "By playing a game? Give me a break." He leaned against the wall with his arms crossed. "I'm going to tell you something about basketball, and I want you to listen very closely."

I groaned.

"You know I was the star player on my high school team, and even got a college scholarship."

"I know, Dad." I'd heard it all before.

"But when I got to college, every guy on the team had been the best in his high school. And some were even the best in their *state*. I played, but not all the time, and I never started."

I'd never heard *that* before. "You didn't?" I asked.

"Nope. And when I graduated, only two of the guys from my college team got drafted into the NBA."

"Who?" I asked. If Dad played ball with a legend like

Charles Barkley or Shaq and never told me, my head was going to explode.

"John Foster and Gary Washington."

"Who?"

"You want to know why you've never heard of them?" he asked, but didn't give me a chance to answer. "John was injured before his first season even started and never played a game."

"Whoa." How much would *that* stink?

"And Gary simply wasn't as good as the other guys on the team. You know how many minutes he played during his two years in the NBA?"

"No."

"Twenty-six."

"*Minutes?*" I winced. Out of eighty-eight games a year? For two years that would be . . . something Russ could probably figure out. A lot, anyway. "Ouch."

"He ended up moving back to Oregon after that. He took over his dad's insurance business and he still runs it with his sister." He was quiet. "You know, some things aren't all they're cracked up to be. You can be at the top of your game and still not make it. And I'm not just talking about basketball."

"You aren't?"

"No. You need to remember that whether you become an NBA player, a doctor, teacher, plumber, or whatever, the only thing that will be the same no matter what is that your family will be there for you. Your brother Russell will always be there when you need him."

I knew he was right. Russ might have outplayed me on the court, but off the court, he'd never let me down.

"Russell will always have your back." Dad paused to give me a long, hard look. "So why don't you have his?"

I didn't go shoot hoops.

I started to, but when I got to the park, I sat on an empty bench instead, with the ball in my lap. How had everything gotten so messed up, so fast? I'd been excited about basketball season all summer long, and only two games in, it was totally wrecked.

Russ thought I was a jerk.

Dad thought I was a rotten brother.

Coach thought I belonged on the bench.

My whole team thought I was a ball hog.

And the worst part? They were all right.

I watched some kids throwing a Frisbee around and tried to figure out how to make everything go back to normal. Back to how things were when everyone liked me.

And then it hit me.

Of course, I knew *one* thing I could fix.

I checked Russ's watch and figured I had time before

dinner, so I started running. I turned onto Sycamore and ran even faster until I got to Lewis and Clark Middle School.

When I made it to the Dumpster, I took a deep breath, then pulled myself up to the rim.

As soon as I looked inside, I wanted to puke.

I'd totally forgotten it was spaghetti day.

All I could see were wet noodles and tomato sauce piled on top of all the other garbage. What if the shoes were covered in old, gross food?

Dad had already said he was going to get Russ new ones, anyway.

I stared at the mess and sighed.

The new shoes weren't the point. I had to get the old ones back, to show Russ I knew I'd made a mistake and that I wasn't really a jerk.

At least not all the time.

I imagined the Nikes when we'd first seen them at the store. The coolest shoes ever. And the look on Russ's face when Dad bought them? Super happy.

Just do it.

I climbed into the Dumpster. The smell was totally sick, and the pile was wet and slippery. I was careful, but as soon as the sole of my shoe touched down, everything went wrong.

"Urgh!" I grunted, as I slipped and fell, banging my elbow hard on the side of the Dumpster before landing in a puddle of sauce. It smelled even worse than it looked.

I jumped to my feet as fast as I could, groaning when I saw the goo all over my shorts. I braced myself against the wall and lifted one shoe to check the damage. Wet noodles were tangled in my laces, and sauce was smeared all over the leather.

Great.

There was nothing I could do about it, so I started moving toward the corner where I'd thrown the shoes. With every step, I wondered if there were rats beneath me. And what kind of rotting cafeteria food made up the next layer down?

Didn't we have mac and cheese this week?

I got my answer when I took the next squishy step.

Yes, we did.

Ugh.

I pushed papers and lunch bags out of the way, and that's when I saw something shiny.

Plastic wrap. And underneath it? A miracle in the shape of a silver swoosh.

I grabbed the first shoe, and the second was right beneath it.

No way!

I held both of them up for inspection.

There was a bit of junk on the soles and a few little blobs of tomato sauce on the sides, but otherwise they were perfect.

What were the chances of a bunch of plastic being thrown into the Dumpster right before the spaghetti? I felt like the luckiest kid on the planet, which was pretty amazing, considering I was covered in cold wet noodles and standing in a giant stinking garbage can.

But I didn't care. When Russ saw the shoes, he'd forgive me.

I wiped off the face of his watch.

Five minutes until dinner!

I climbed out of the Dumpster and sprinted all the way home, hugging the dirty shoes against my chest. Every time my feet hit the pavement, they sprayed spaghetti sauce. Russ's shoes might have been in good condition, but mine were toast.

I was pretty sure that served me right.

When I got back to the house, I had a cramp in my side and I was totally out of breath. I walked into the kitchen, where Mom, Dad, and Russ were sitting at the table.

"You made it," Mom said, without looking up.

"Whoa! What happened to you?" Dad choked.

"Nothing. I mean, I went to get Russ's shoes and—"

Mom glanced up from her food and froze. "What on earth?"

"I got them!" I held up the shoes for everyone to see. "There's barely anything on them, so they're practically good as new. See, Russ?"

I walked toward him, but Mom jumped up from her seat. "Hold on, Owen. I don't want you tracking that all over the house. You're absolutely covered." She stared at me. "What happened?"

"I fell in a Dumpster. I mean, I was already in it when I fell down."

"He threw the shoes in there," Russ said quietly.

Mom looked from Russ to me, trying to figure out if he was kidding. "But why would Owen—"

"I got them back," I interrupted, focusing on my brother. "They're just like new, Russ. I'll clean them up and they'll be perfect." I held them up so he could check them out. "See?"

"I see," he said. He pushed back his chair to get up from the table.

"Where are you going?" Mom asked.

"To my room," he said.

"Still not feeling good?" she asked.

"No," he said, and left the kitchen.

"I have no idea what's going on here," Mom said, "but I don't like it."

I didn't like it either. Russ was supposed to forgive me.

"You know you still have to mow the lawn, right?" Dad asked me.

I nodded. "I know."

"And we're still going to get Russ another pair."

"Yes, and I want to, Dad. I just thought if he saw I was trying, he might—"

Dad nodded. "It may take some more time and effort." He rested a hand on the clean part of my sleeve. "But that was a good start."

"It was?" I asked, relieved.

"It was, and I'm proud of you, Owen."

"Thanks, Dad."

"Now please go hose yourself off."

Russell skipped the next basketball practice and when everyone asked about him, I said he was sick. He wasn't, though. He was hanging out with the Masters of the Mind team instead.

"Great, so we're stuck with the ball hog," Paul groaned.

"Look, I know I hogged the ball and—"

"Made some lame shots?" Nate asked.

"Some good ones, too," I told him. "But yeah, I made some lame ones."

"Why didn't you pass?" Paul asked.

"I don't know," I told him. "I mean, I was just trying to show off and it backfired."

"Yup," Nate said.

"Come on," Chris said. "He's trying to say he's sorry."

"Then say it," Paul said, glaring at me.

I looked from one guy to the next, staring each of them right in the eye so they'd know I meant it. "I'm really sorry, guys. It won't happen again."

"That's what I like to hear," Coach Baxter said, clapping his hands. "In basketball, you lose enough guys to injuries. I'd hate to lose one to ego."

"You won't," I told him. "I'm sorry, Coach."

"Hey, you're passionate about the game," he said, patting me on the back. "And that's a good thing. You just can't let the passion rule everything else."

Russ didn't go to the next practice either, and every time I tried to talk to him about basketball, he walked away.

When I invited him to watch a game on TV, he shook his head and went upstairs. When I asked him to pass the potatoes at the dinner table, he handed them over without even looking at me. I even tried asking him questions about science, just to get him talking, but even that didn't work.

The house felt quiet and lonely.

I missed my brother, and he was right there in front of me.

"We have a game today," I reminded him on Friday morning.

He didn't care.

But the rest of us did. Parkrose Middle School was a good team, and we Pioneers had our work cut out for us.

Chris, Paul, and I met outside the school after the final bell and waited for the rest of the guys.

"So, are we going to take the Pacers down?" Paul asked.

I shrugged.

"Is Russ coming?"

"Nope," I said, shaking my head.

"Nuts." Paul sighed. "We need him."

"I know. Look, I've tried talking to him, but he won't listen."

"What happened?" Chris asked, for, like, the tenth time.

I didn't want anyone to know how much of a jerk I'd been. If the guys found out that it was totally my fault that Russ was bailing on basketball, they'd hate me.

"No idea," I lied. "I think he's busy with school."

Luckily, the rest of the guys showed up so we could stop talking and get going.

"No Russell?" Coach asked, checking names on his clipboard as each of us climbed onto the bus.

"No," I told him.

Coach put his hand on my shoulder to stop me. "Do you think he'll come back?"

"I hope so," I said. And it was true. I missed Russ more

than I ever thought I could. At home, at school, *and* on the basketball court.

"Do what you can to convince him."

"I will," I told him, and went to find a seat.

"We're going to have to work our butts off," Chris said when I sat next to him. "These guys are good, and without Russ—"

"We're the underdog," I finished for him.

"Yeah," Chris said, biting his lip. "We are."

"But underdogs have won before," I reminded him.

"I guess," Chris said doubtfully.

"I have a feeling we're going to win," I told him. "And I mean win big."

We lost.

And I mean lost big.

They killed us. Right from the start, it was like they were in high school and we were in kindergarten.

Their players were the same size as us, but twice as fast, so it always felt like they outnumbered us on the court.

Paul had eight turnovers . . . in the first half! Chris had three fouls and no points. Nate missed two free throws, right when we needed them.

And me? I passed the ball and tried to do the right thing

whenever I could, but I'd only scored six points by the end of the game.

"That was brutal," Chris moaned on the bus ride home.

"That's what practice is for," Coach said. "And boys, we *will* be practicing."

RUSSELL

Perfect Symmetry

I knew that skipping practices wasn't fair to Coach or my teammates, but I did it, anyway.

I'm sure Owen thought that returning my spaghetti shoes and half apologizing was going to make everything okay between us, but he was wrong.

I had a lot to sort out in my mind, and it seemed like the best way to do that was to forget about basketball until I took care of everything else.

It was time for some changes.

The first thing that needed changing was my homework and study schedule, which had disappeared when basketball took over. I spent a couple of nights getting up to speed for all my classes, and I could feel my shoulders start to relax.

Next up was Masters of the Mind, but I had no idea how to repair my relationship with the group. Arthur Richardson the Third was ruining the team, and my gut instinct was to get rid of him.

But how?

The team was open to everyone, we weren't over the limit for members, his donut sales paid our entry fees for the district challenge, *and* he'd had a lot of good ideas for competition.

But, just like my brother, he was a real jerk.

× ÷ +

Nitu and I walked to Sunset Park together on the next game day. We ended up at the basketball court, which was empty.

"That's where the whole mess got started," I told her.

She glanced at me. "I heard you've been skipping basketball practices."

I shrugged. "Yeah. And a game tonight."

She frowned at me. "That's not like you, Russell. You're not a skipper."

"I am now, I guess."

"The coach won't let you do that for long, you know. He'll kick you off the team."

"Maybe that would be a good thing," I said, and sighed.

She turned to stare at me. "Come on, Russell. You don't mean that."

"Why not? It's caused me nothing but trouble."

"But you love it."

"No, I don't."

"Russell," she said, raising one eyebrow at me. "You're almost as happy being on the Pioneers as you are in Masters of the Mind."

"No, I—"

She raised a finger to stop me. "I said *almost*."

"Even if you're right, it doesn't matter, Nitu. The two things just don't work together."

"Says who?" asked my favorite math whiz.

"Sara and Jason." I sighed. "Arthur Richardson the Third."

"He doesn't count," she said, and snorted. "And the other two? They're just scared, so they're following his lead."

"Basketball." I groaned. "It's ruining everything. I can't even be around my brother anymore."

"Why not?" Nitu asked, looking surprised.

I told her what happened with the Nikes and she shook her head.

"He shouldn't have done that."

"You're telling me?"

"You need to talk to him about it."

"I can't, Nitu. I'm so mad, I just—"

"He's your brother, Russell. There are billions of people on this planet and out of all of them, only one is your brother."

"I know." I sighed, hating that she was right.

"Talk to him, Russell."

"No." I had to put myself first, for once.

✖ ➗ ➕

Later that afternoon, I was reading ahead in my social studies textbook when Mom knocked on my door.

"Can I come in?"

"Sure."

I smiled when she opened the door, but that smile shrunk when she sat down on the bed. It wasn't looking like a quick visit, and I wanted to get through those chapters.

"How are things going?" she asked.

"Fine. I'm learning about the wonders of ancient Greece."

"Sounds good," she said, then cleared her throat. "So, I've noticed a bit of a chill in the air between you and your brother. Your dad filled me in on the shoes and the rest of what he knows. Do you want to talk about it?"

I must have wanted to, because even though I had work to do, I ended up telling her everything. I started with my fear of trying out for the team and the surprise of enjoying basketball. Then I talked about Owen wanting me to fail and the horrible feeling that I'd let down the Masters team while Arthur tried to take over as team leader.

"*Whew,*" she said when I was finished. "And that's all happened in the past couple of weeks?"

"Yes." I sighed.

"Honey, it's not good for you to keep all this stress and worry inside."

"I know. Stress can cause high blood pressure and—" I began.

She looked like she was trying not to laugh. "That wasn't exactly my point, Russell."

"What was it, then?"

"Stress can take a lot of the fun out of childhood. You're young and you should be enjoying yourself."

"I *do* enjoy myself," I assured her. "It's just been harder than usual lately."

"Well, I think the place to start is to patch things up with Owen."

"Mom," I groaned.

She sounded just like Nitu.

"I'm serious. I know he did some terrible things, but do you think he actually feels good about them?"

I didn't have to think about that for more than a second. "I'm sure he doesn't."

"So?"

"So, it's not my job to make him feel better, Mom. He betrayed me."

"I'll let you stew on that for a bit," she said, standing up. "He may not show it all the time, but he loves you and he'll always be your brother."

When she left me alone, I didn't know what to think.

× ÷ +

Later that evening, while Owen was still at the game, Nitu and Sara showed up at my house.

"Did you talk to Owen?" Nitu asked, once we were in the privacy of my room.

"He's not home yet."

"But you will when he gets back, right?"

"No," I told her, as I pulled out the books I'd need for English class the next day.

"Then when will you?"

"Maybe in a year or two."

She put her hands on her hips. "Well, they aren't going to reschedule the district challenge if you stress yourself into some kind of a breakdown."

"Breakdown?" Sara asked, sounding worried as she looked from Nitu to me.

"I'm not having a breakdown," I told her. But when I thought about it, I realized Nitu wasn't *that* far off. "It's more like an identity crisis."

Nitu raised an eyebrow at me. "Are you really trying to decide whether you're a basketball player or a Master of the Mind?"

"Yes." And whether I'd accidentally taken over Owen's role as the family athlete. Maybe he was having an identity crisis, too.

If I was the athlete *and* the mathlete, what did that leave for him?

Nitu looked worried. "Are you thinking about quitting?"

"Yes," I said, trying to imagine how it would feel to turn in my jersey and what I would say to Coach Baxter.

"What?" Sara gasped.

"No, no." I shook my head. "Not Masters. I'm thinking about quitting *basketball*."

"*Whew.*" Sara smiled. "You were making me nervous."

"Do you know what's making *me* nervous?" I asked, ready to talk about something other than sports or my brother. "I don't know what to do about Arthur."

"Neither do we," Sara said, and sighed.

"Why does he even want to be on the team if he doesn't like any of us?" I asked, shaking my head.

Nitu laughed. "You didn't hear why he joined?"

I shook my head. "No."

"Because he thought it would look good on his Harvard application."

"What? We're only in seventh grade!" I choked.

Should I have been thinking about college applications?

I had been, of course, but I hadn't joined clubs or teams based on whether universities would like me for it.

I joined because I wanted to have fun.

"He doesn't really care about any of it," Nitu continued.

"How do you know that?" I asked.

"He told us at the last meeting," Sara explained.

"But he wants to take over as team leader?" I asked.

"Team leader probably looks better on the application." Nitu shrugged.

Knowing that the team meant nothing to Arthur Richardson the Third was enough to convince me that something really had to be done.

And I needed the help of someone villainous.

Luckily, my evil twin lived right down the hall.

Squaring Up

When I got home, my parents asked how the game had gone, and I had to tell them we lost by thirty-two points.

"A blowout." Dad groaned.

"Yup."

"It happens to everyone," he said, patting me on the back.

"Once?"

"More than once," he said with a laugh. "It's sad, but true."

It was sad, all right. "We really needed Russ."

"Then you should tell him," Mom said, like that was the easiest thing in the world.

Had she been in the same house as us for the past few days? Had she seen Russ pretend I didn't even exist?

"Uh, he's not talking to me."

"That's the best part of telling him how you feel," Mom said. "All he has to do is listen."

But was Russ going to listen to me after I'd been such a jerk? I mean, what would I have done if he'd thrown my brand-new shoes in the Dumpster?

I would have given him something a lot worse than the silent treatment.

"Just try, honey," Mom said while she messed up my hair. "It's all you can do."

I figured she was right, so I climbed the stairs and knocked on Russ's bedroom door.

"Come in," I heard from inside.

I turned the knob and opened it.

My brother was sitting at his desk, doing homework. He looked disappointed when he saw my face. "Oh, it's you."

"Yeah," I said, going in, anyway.

His Nikes were sitting on the floor of his closet. I hadn't seen him wear them since Dumpster Day. The new box (with the even better and more expensive shoes Dad bought for him) was still in the Go Time bag. "So, we uh—"

"I'm trying to study, Owen."

If he wasn't studying, he was reading. If he wasn't reading, he was brainstorming. He could have used any excuse not to talk to me and he had. *For days.*

"I know, but—"

"It's what I do." He frowned. "I study, I get good grades, I read nerdy books for fun, and I hang out with geeks, because I am one."

"No you're not," I told him. "Well, you are . . . but not in a bad way."

"Of course I am, and it was stupid of me to think I could be anything else."

"No it wasn't, Russ."

He sighed, and turned back to his books. "I'm too busy for this."

"We lost tonight," I told him.

"Too bad," he said, without looking at me.

"It was, actually. We got smoked."

Russ flipped a page, then glanced at me again. "Are you still here?"

I wasn't going anywhere. "We lost by thirty-two points."

"And?" He shrugged and looked at his book again.

I knew he was only pretending to read, though. His eyes weren't even moving. And that meant I had his attention! But what should I say to keep it?

The truth.

"And we needed you."

That snapped him out of it. He lifted his head from the book but still didn't make eye contact. He stared at his map of stars and stuff instead.

And then I went for it.

"We really did, Russ. We needed you to block, because no one else can do it like you—"

"I just stand there," he said, quietly.

"No, you don't, and you know it. You block shots like crazy. We needed you for that, we needed you for points—"

"I can't make free throws."

"But you can make *jump shots*."

"My layups are really bad."

"So? You make up for it in three-pointers."

"I'm slow."

He had me there. "Uh . . . you're getting faster." At least I hoped he was.

"Look, I—"

"No, *you* look," I said. "Seriously, Russ. Look at me."

He turned toward me and fixed his crooked glasses. "What?"

"We need you on the team."

He shook his head. "But you don't—"

"*I* need you on the team."

He didn't say anything for a few seconds. "Really?"

"Really. I'm sorry I was such a jerk, but I was . . ." It was hard to say, but I had to do it. "I was jealous."

Russ's eyes got huge. "Of me?"

"Yes," I said, and gulped.

"Of my *basketball playing*?"

"Yup."

He leaned back in his chair. "That's so weird."

"Why?"

He shook his head, like the question was nuts. "No one has ever been jealous of me before, Owen. About anything. Not my math awards, my honor roll standing, and especially not sports."

• "Well, I was." I cleared my throat. "I want to show you something, Russ."

"I—"

Before he could say anything, I pulled my "inspiration" paper from my back pocket. I'd given up on writing about Tim Camden when I saw what playing like him had done to me and my team. It made them almost hate me, even when I scored. And how "inspiring" was a ball hog, anyway?

It had taken me a while to come up with a better subject for my paper, but that was okay. I'd had lots of time to think when Russ wasn't talking to me, and I'd figured out that my inspiration was . . . him.

I'd been feeling a bit weird about showing the paper to my brother, but I needed him to know how I felt. How important he was to me. How even though I was thirteen minutes older, I looked up to him.

I took a deep breath.

"Look," I said, handing him the paper.

Russ squinted at it, then smiled. "An A-plus? That's great, Owen!"

"No, I mean . . . read it."

"Your paper?"

"Yeah."

My hands sweat and I tried not to watch him.

"You spelled 'fraternal' wrong," he said half a second after he started reading.

"Geez. Don't *correct* it; *read* it."

Luckily, it only took him a minute or so.

When he was done, his face was pink and he was smiling. "Thank you, Owen."

"You like it?" I asked nervously.

"Definitely." He nodded, then asked, "You really feel that way about me?"

"Yeah, I do."

"Wow," he whispered. "So, does this mean you're not jealous of me anymore?" He sounded kind of disappointed.

"Maybe a little bit, but I'll get over it. And I already know how."

"How?"

That was easy.

I had a brand-new plan, and it was better than being the go-to guy. It was better than being selfish about scoring or greedy about gear. And it was definitely better than getting smoked by thirty-two points.

My brand-new plan was all about teamwork.

"Look, you've got skills and I've got skills. Separately, we're good, but together, along with the rest of the Pioneers . . . we're dangerous."

"But when you and I played together before—"

"That was before," I told him. "From now on, two Evans brothers on the court at the same time is going to be . . ." I searched for the right word and it only took me a second to find it. "Magical."

"You think so?" Russ asked doubtfully.

"Totally."

He didn't say anything right away and I hoped what I'd said was sinking in. I didn't know what else I could do to convince him.

Finally, he nodded. "I'll think about it."

"Awesome!"

"I said I'll *think about it.*"

"I know," I told him. "I'm cool with that."

I couldn't believe how happy I was that we were talking again. For the first time ever, I actually felt like my brother was my friend. It was amazing.

I hung out in Russ's room for a little while after that, and we talked about stuff we'd never gone over before.

One of those things was this twerp on his Masters of the Mind team named Arthur Richardson the Third. It turned out the kid had been kind of pushing my brother around and trying to take over.

And I'd had no idea.

Russell told me all about it, and when he was done, I had only one thing to say.

"Give him peanuts."

"What?" Russ asked, blinking hard.

"You said he told you guys that peanuts are like grenades to him, so—"

"Owen," Russell interrupted, shaking his head. "I don't want to *kill* him."

Geez. Did he want my help or not? "Okay, what if you fed him something and just told him there were peanuts in it?" I suggested.

Russ looked at me like I was crazy. "What would that do?"

"Freak him out for a few minutes, which would be awesome to watch."

Russell shook his head again. "I don't think we're attacking this from the right angle. Just forget the peanuts for now, okay?"

I nodded, and we were both quiet while we thought of a way to get rid of him.

"What's the college he wants to go to?" I asked.

"Harvard."

I was pretty sure I'd heard of it before. "Where's that?"

Russ stared at me like I'd just asked him what my own name was. "Are you joking?"

"No." Was it *that* dumb a question?

He looked like he wanted to say something, but he cleared his throat instead. Finally, he told me, "It's in Massachusetts."

"Okay. Do they have any big teams or anything?"

"Are we talking about sports?"

"Yeah."

"They're the Crimson, Owen. They have teams for everything, but I think they're known for rowing."

"That works. And what about these college applications Arthur talks about? Do they want kids to be total brains and that's it?"

He thought for a second. "I've never looked at one, but I've always heard it's important to be well-rounded."

"Like, fat?"

"What?" He looked confused for a second, then sighed. "Well-rounded means interested in more than one thing."

"Like playing basketball *and* baseball?"

"No." He sighed again, and I could tell this Arthur kid had really gotten on his nerves. "Like basketball and . . . let's say singing."

"A singing basketball player?" I asked. "That doesn't even make sense."

"Okay, a singing basketball player who's also part of a science or book club."

"Gotcha," I said, nodding as an idea came to me. "So, if you let Arthur know that being a brainiac isn't going to guarantee he gets into Havard—"

"Harvard," Russ corrected.

"Right, Harvard. Anyway, if he starts to think that one more nerdy club won't mean as much as playing a sport—"

"Or volunteering somewhere," Russ said, and I could tell by his smile that he was getting it.

"Yeah," I told him. "Put enough pressure on being 'well-rounded' and he'll quit on his own."

"You really think so?" Russ asked.

I rolled my eyes. "Why did you ask me to help?"

"Because I thought you were . . ." He stopped, looking uncomfortable.

"You can say it."

"Because I thought you were evil."

"Evil?" I choked. "Okay, I was thinking of something more like crafty, but I guess 'evil' fits."

"Not every day or anything," he rushed to say. "Just sometimes."

"Gotcha," I said. "Anyway, you've got to trust me. The only way you're going to get rid of this kid is by peanuts—"

"Owen . . . ," he warned me.

"Or by outsmarting him." I smiled. "And Russ, you're not just smart, you're a freaking genius."

RUSSELL

Bonding Energy

On the day before our district challenge, I rounded up the rest of the Masters of the Mind team and explained Owen's plan.

"You really think it will work?" Sara asked doubtfully.

Nitu slowly nodded. "He won't want to be part of the team if he thinks he'll look better doing something else."

"When are we going to do this?" Sara asked.

"Tomorrow morning," I told her.

"What?" Sara gasped. "But the district challenge—"

"We've got to take care of this," I told the group. "The sooner the better." It was great to feel like a leader again. And I owed that feeling to my brother.

"I'm with Russell," Nitu said.

"Me, too." Jason smiled. "Maybe we're not doomed, after all."

The rest of the school day was, as Owen would say, awesome.

I scored 98 percent on my math test and got an A on my social studies report. Everything felt like it was back on track, and my focus was right where it should be.

But at the same time, I missed basketball. I missed the blast of Coach's whistle, the roar of the crowd, and the feeling that we Pioneers were in it together. I missed the squeak of my Nikes against the floor and the sight of my twin racing down the court.

"So play," Nitu said when I told her how I felt. "Owen practically begged you to go back to the team, didn't he?"

"Yes, but there's the practice schedule, games, my Masters commitments, homework, Math Club. Basketball takes a lot of time, and—"

"Russell," she interrupted. "You're a professional problem solver. Figure it out."

So I did. I sat down during my lunch hour and made up a weekly schedule. Once I saw all the practices, games, and meetings in print, I also saw how much space there was around them. I *did* have time to do it all. I just needed to organize myself a little better.

I felt a smile appear on my face.

I would be a Pioneer again.

✗ ÷ +

The next morning, I woke up excited about the district competition. If everything went according to plan, in a couple of hours Arthur would be off the team and we'd be on our way to Regionals.

My bag was already packed for the trip to the community center, so I climbed into the van with everything I needed, including schematics and tons of notes.

"Move over," Owen grunted, climbing in next to me.

"What are you doing?" I asked him.

"I'm coming." He shrugged, buckling his seat belt.

"Coming where?" I asked.

"The meet," Dad said, opening the front passenger door. "Masters of the Mind."

"You're coming?" I gasped.

"We want to see you in action," Owen said, elbowing me.

I couldn't believe it! No one but Mom had ever watched Masters before. "Seriously?"

"Seriously," Owen said.

$$\times \quad \div \quad +$$

When we got to River Glen Community Center, I caught up with Sara at the front door.

"Nervous?" I asked, pulling it open for her.

"A little," she whispered.

The gym had been divided into sections. There was a

large space with tables and chairs for teams to be tested on word or math problems, and the rest was split into eight smaller areas, one for each competing school. Those areas each had a table and a cardboard box filled with all the ingredients on our challenge lists, checked and measured to make sure everything was fair. Teams weren't allowed to bring anything but paperwork in there.

We would prepare for the egg drop at the table, closely watched by judges.

I glanced down at my schematic, wishing we'd had a little more time to test our design.

"There they are!" I heard Nitu call over the sound of the crowd. "Russ! Sara! We're over here!"

We joined them under the Lewis and Clark Middle School sign that marked our territory.

"Ready?" I asked, looking from one face to the next.

"Yup," Jason said, waving to his dad in the stands.

"Absolutely." Nitu nodded. "My whole family is here."

"Mine, too," I said, grinning.

"Can we just get down to business?" Arthur asked.

I exchanged a look with Nitu. "Uh, sure."

Jason and I left to register at the front desk while the others went over our plans.

"Arthur's mad because his dad sent the donut guy to watch instead of coming himself."

I stared at him. "He sent his personal assistant?"

When Jason nodded, I felt sorry for Arthur.

But that didn't last for long.

"Because it's stupid," I heard him saying, when we returned to the team.

"What's stupid?" I asked.

"Our design." He sniffed. "Jason's design. It will never work."

"It worked at practice," Nitu reminded him.

"Once," he growled.

"Let's focus on preparing for the word problems right now," I said. "We're up in fifteen minutes."

The five of us sat on the floor in a circle, but only four of us knew what we were going to do.

"You know, Arthur, I was thinking about what you said about university applications the other day," Nitu said, after the first two practice rounds. "It turns out that my mom's friend can help me get into volunteering at the hospital."

Before Arthur could say anything, Sara said, "That's a really good idea. I've heard that universities love volunteer work."

"Me, too," I said, nodding.

"Art, too," Sara continued. "I'm sure I'll be mentioning my pottery and painting when the time comes."

Right on cue, Jason joined in. "I'm too busy with this team and music to do much else."

It was my turn again, according to the script we'd come

up with. "But marching band will be great for your application."

And just as we'd rehearsed, I put the nail in Arthur's coffin.

"Don't you think it's unfair that we're supposed to be so well-rounded?" I asked the group. "We spend so much time studying and working on academic stuff . . . I think academics should count for more."

"But they don't," Jason said, then sighed.

"That's why I think it's so cool you're playing basketball now, Russell," Sara added. "You're a double threat."

"Double threat?" Arthur asked, looking worried.

"You know, brains and brawn," Nitu said, with a smile I knew was fake. "Like a Harvard medical student who's also captain of the rugby team."

"Good point," Arthur said softly. "Brains *and* brawn."

We carried on for a few more minutes, just for fun, and I watched Arthur look more and more uncomfortable.

And distracted.

"How about some more practice problems?" I asked.

Sara flipped through the pages until she found some new ones. "Okay, it's a name game. Personal names that are linked to careers. The example is Rose Bush. She's a gardener."

"Puns," Nitu said, with a smile.

We had one minute to brainstorm and two minutes to answer.

Finally, I could focus on the task at hand, instead of on Arthur Richardson the Third. It felt amazing.

"Time," Sara said, holding up her stopwatch after sixty seconds.

"I've got one," Nitu said. "Sue Neighbors. She's a lawyer."

"Ally Gator," Sara said. "A veterinarian."

"Nice one," I said, smiling. "How about Cliff Hanger, mountain climber?"

Jason laughed. "I like it. Jack Hammer, construction worker."

"Good!" Nitu said. "Bill Board. He's in advertising, like my dad."

"Clara Nett," Sara piped up. "Professional musician."

"Perfect," I told her, loving all the ideas. "I've got one inspired by the Pioneers. Jim Floor. He's a basketball coach."

"Ha!" Nitu laughed, then glanced at Arthur, who had been totally silent. "What about you?"

Arthur stared at the notes in front of him.

"Arthur?" Jason asked. "Have you got anything?"

He blinked a couple of times, like he was waking up. "No."

"Nothing?" I asked, surprised.

Arthur cleared his throat. "I must have missed the instructions." He glanced at Sara. "Your voice is too quiet."

Of course, her voice was fine. The truth was, we'd scared Arthur enough that he'd stopped listening.

"You've got *something* on your notepad," Jason said, pointing.

"It's nothing," he said, looking uncomfortable.

"Just tell us," Nitu said, with a shrug.

Arthur sighed with frustration. "Louis Zurcitti."

"I don't get it," Jason said.

I didn't either.

"He's my father's accountant."

"I still don't get it," Nitu said, shaking her head.

Arthur's face turned red. "It isn't a pun. It's just the name of a real person. I misunderstood, all right?"

In a couple of seconds, he'd packed up his things and told us he had somewhere he needed to be.

"But we're about to *compete*," I reminded him.

"Forget it," he snapped, and walked away.

When he was gone, we quietly cheered, then Sara started giggling.

"What?" I asked.

"I shouldn't say it. It's not very nice."

"Go for it," Nitu urged her.

"The name he gave." She started giggling again, pointing at the notepad Arthur had left behind. "I think it was Arthur's destination."

We all stared at her, confused.

"If you shorten Louis to Lou, it's Lou Zurcitti."

"Loser City," Jason snorted.

The Masters of the Mind team cracked up.

We'd rid ourselves of Arthur and soon it was time to do the rest.

Our brains were warmed up for the judges, and we raced through three problems like they were nothing.

"Nice work, guys!" I said as we left the testing area. "I have a good feeling about this."

"Me, too," Nitu said, grinning. "Right now, I have a good feeling about . . . everything!" She paused for a second to think. "No matter how the challenge ends, I'm happy to be here with friends."

Glad we were back to rhyming, I chimed in with, "When they put us to the test, we can only do our best."

And Sara added, "If we don't win, have no fear, we'll have another chance next year."

We all looked to Jason, who smiled and shrugged as he told us. "I know that I'm supposed to grin, but honestly, I'd rather win."

And we all cracked up again.

We checked the scoreboard an hour later and saw that we were tied with Beaumont for first place.

When it was time for the egg-drop challenge, we moved to our assigned area. The cardboard box filled with ingredients sat waiting for us.

We knew that two things had to happen for us to win the district competition:

1. Our egg had to land in perfect condition.
2. Beaumont's had to crack or break.

Before I could think about it too much, the Beaumont team formed a huddle and started chanting something I could barely hear.

I glanced at my teammates, who looked worried.

I thought of the Pioneers and put one hand out between us. Jason looked confused until I signaled for him to put his hand in as well. The girls did the same.

"Okay," I said. "Lewis and Clark on three."

"On three what?" Nitu asked.

"When I say three," I told her.

"Why are you saying three?" Sara asked.

I shook my head. "Just shout Lewis and Clark when you hear it," I told her, then took a deep breath. "One, two . . . three."

"Lewis and Clark!" we all shouted at once.

We were ready.

And so were the other teams, the judges, and our audience. So, when all the competitors were in their positions, we got started.

In practice, we'd tried my net idea, but it turned out to work much better in my head than it did in real life. It had only taken four broken eggs to convince me that we needed to try something new.

Since a good leader knows that the best ideas aren't always his own, we'd chosen Jason's plan.

And now we had to make it work in front of an audience.

The seconds ticked quietly on an egg timer as we put our carrier together. There were excited voices all around us as the other teams did the same.

Jason duct-taped the edges of our newspaper pages so they wouldn't tear while Nitu molded the aluminum-foil basket that would carry the egg. I cut our string into four equal pieces, then cut holes in the corners of the newspaper pages. Sara threaded the string through the holes and tied them to the handle of the foil basket.

We had our parachute.

"Less than a minute left," Jason said, watching the clock.

"Styrofoam," Nitu said.

As quickly as we could, we broke our chunks into tiny pieces, then filled our foil basket with them.

Sara placed our egg on top of the Styrofoam and Nitu secured a layer of foil over the top.

We all glanced at each other and nodded.

We were finished.

There was frantic scrambling all around us until the buzzer went off.

It was time!

Most of the competitors moved outside with the audience while Sara and one member from each of the other teams carried the eggs upstairs.

In just a few minutes, the first egg came sailing toward the ground . . . and smashed onto the pavement.

The crowd gasped.

I guess the chopsticks were a bad idea.

Two more eggs splattered, then another three.

When our turn finally came, not a single egg had made it.

I took a deep breath as Sara released the newspaper parachute into the sky above us. It swayed a few feet, pushed by the breeze. I was worried the basket would tip, but let go of the breath when it straightened out.

"Please, please, please," Nitu whispered.

"It's slower than any of the others," I said. "That's a good sign."

When the parachute landed, the judge made sure the egg had no cracks.

"Lewis and Clark Middle School is in first place."

We would have cheered, but Beaumont was still waiting for their turn.

I held my breath again when their egg carrier was dropped from the window. It looked like it was moving too fast, but it was hard to know for sure.

When it landed, the judge examined the egg even more carefully than she'd checked ours.

"Just a crack," Jason whispered. "One little crack."

"Please, please, please," our math whiz whispered again.

I would have crossed my fingers, begged and pleaded for one little crack, too, but I suddenly realized that wasn't what I wanted. At all.

"What's wrong, Russ?" Nitu asked.

I shook my head. "I don't want to win like this."

She gasped. "Like what?"

I looked at all the smug Beaumont faces lined up across from us. "I don't want the judges to need a magnifying glass to declare us the winners, Nitu. I don't want to *squeak* into first place."

"A win is a win, Russell."

"No," I said, looking right at Peter and thinking about the Pioneers' thirty-two-point loss. A *blowout*. "No, I want our win to be so huge and obvious it's visible from *space*."

"What?"

Before I could answer, the judge announced, "Perfect condition! Ladies and gentlemen, we have a tie."

"Excellent," I said, grinning. "That means we get to compete against them at Regionals."

My teammates and I rushed over to the Beaumont team to congratulate them on our joint win.

"We're going to stomp you next time," Peter said, with a cold smile. "Trust me."

"Whoa," Jason whispered.

I led the team back to our area, already feeling excited about the rematch. "Okay, we've got one month until Regionals. We're going to need to find our fifth team member within the next few days," I said to the group. "Agreed?"

"Agreed," they all answered at once.

I don't know whether it was the influence of my evil twin or the competition on the basketball court, but I surprised myself by adding, "Because we've got to *destroy* Beaumont."

I glanced at Nitu and saw that I'd surprised her, too. Not to mention Jason and Sara, whose mouths were hanging open.

"Well," I said, clearing my throat, "beat them, anyway."

Jason laughed. "I'm with you, Russ."

"We're going to Regionals!" Nitu screamed, pulling us all into a hug.

We couldn't stop laughing.

And the next thing I knew, my whole family had gathered around us.

I never would have imagined it, but Mom, Dad, and Owen were right there with me, standing in the middle of the Masters of the Mind district competition, hugging me and cheering like we'd won a championship basketball game.

It felt . . . magical.

Nothing but Net

At the next Pioneers game, the crowd went crazy. The bleachers were packed and the team was on fire. Russ and I were out on the court together, right where we belonged.

It felt so good to have my brother back. I kept checking to make sure he was really there, but he'd already put sixteen points on the board to prove it.

After what happened on the court before, Coach hadn't been too sure about putting the Evans brothers in together, but we were proving that it was the right move.

People had always asked me if my twin and I could read each other's minds, and I'd laughed. But during that game, we were so in sync, it was scary.

And awesome.

When we got down to the last minute or so of the final quarter, the Pioneers were losing by just one stinkin' point. I knew we could take the game if we just played smart.

I ran down the court.

Just one basket to win it!

I dribbled around one guard, then another, while the crowd cheered. It was the kind of moment I'd always dreamed about. I got into position and lined up the shot. Then I saw Russ out of the corner of my eye. He was wide open, just standing there.

I didn't even have to think about what I did next.

I passed him the ball.

Russ looked surprised, catching it at the same time the two guards went after him. He went vertical to make his jump shot, but at the very last second, he twisted in midair and passed the ball back to *me*.

I couldn't believe it! After everything that had happened, Russ was willing to share the glory.

I aimed for the basket and let go of the ball.

Swish.

The crowd were on their feet, screaming like lunatics, and so were the Pioneers.

We won!

I grinned as I ran over to Russ, and he grinned right back at me.

We'd won the game together, as real teammates, for the first time ever.

I lifted my hand for a high five.

As usual, my brother missed.

But that's okay. It's kind of his trademark now.

Acknowledgments

As always, huge thanks to my agent, Sally Harding, the ultimate literary referee.

And to the Bloomsbury folks, especially Michelle Nagler, who took possession at the tip-off, and Brett Wright, MVP.